The Tw

Jonathan Gathorne-Hardy was born in Edinburgh, and worked for seventeen years at numerous part-time jobs – teacher, book-seller, publisher, reviewer and advertising copy-writer – before the publication of *The Rise and Fall of the British Nanny* enabled him to take up writing full-time. He has written non-fiction and fiction books for both adults and children. He lives in Norfolk with his second wife, the painter Nicky Loutit, and spends his time writing.

Also by Jonathan Gathorne-Hardy

Jane's Adventures In and Out of the Book
Jane's Adventures on the Island of Peeg
Jane's Adventures in a Balloon
The Terrible Kidnapping of Cyril Bonhamy
Cyril Bonhamy V Madam Big
Cyril Bonhamy and the Great Drain Robbery
Cyril Bonhamy and Operation Ping
Cyril of the Apes

and for younger children

The Tunnel Party
The Munro's New House

Jonathan Gathorne-Hardy

The Twin
Detectives

MACMILLAN
CHILDREN'S BOOKS

First published 1995 by Macmillan Children's Books

a division of Macmillan Publishers Limited
25 Eccleston Place London SW1W 9NF
and Basingstoke

Associated companies throughout the world

ISBN 0 330 33271 6

1 3 5 7 9 8 6 4 2

A CIP catalogue record for this book is available from
the British Library

Phototypeset by Intype, London
Printed by Mackays of Chatham PLC, Kent

Contents

To my granddaughter Nell

CHAPTER ONE

"Suppose a dead body came rolling down?"

Kate Anderson was woken by a sudden terrifying scream and then the voice of her twin sister, Sel, crying out, "Kate! Kate! Help me."

She sat up in the darkness and reached across to the sleeping bag next to her own. "It's all right, Sel," she said.

"They were chasing us," said Sel in a thick voice.

As she said it, Kate felt goose-flesh run in a shiver down her back and a strange scene suddenly jumped into her head. She was skimming at tremendous speed over a carpet of light.

"You mean you were flying?" she said. "Flying over light?"

"Flying over light," said Sel, but Kate could feel her sister already falling asleep again. "They were chasing us," she muttered.

For some time afterwards Kate lay awake in the stuffy little tent. She and Sel were identical twins and quite often found they were thinking the same

1

things, and sometimes even dreaming them. This was not the first time she had had a glimpse of one of Sel's nightmares. But she felt sure Sel had not really been dreaming about flying.

Earlier that day Monty Goody, their mother's extremely rich uncle, who lived in the old Rectory in their village in Kent and was paying for the whole family's holiday, had taken the twins on an expedition to Sangatte. Here he had put them on the famous CFMS or *Chemin de Fer Miniature de Sangatte* – the Sangatte miniature railway.

This was a tiny steam train which puffed beside the sea from its station in the middle of Sangatte to Cap Gris-Nez and back. The engine driver had been very excited by the twins. "Tweens!" he had cried. "*Les jumelles anglaises.*" And he had taken them both up beside him in the tiny engine.

Kate had loved it. She had been allowed to drive and had blown the whistle. Sel had simply sat on the coal tender and been frightened.

For some reason, Kate was quite sure her sister's dream had been about the Sangatte miniature railway.

●

The following day was spent packing and tidying up. Shortly after their late lunch in the caravan, Sylvia Anderson had said she could get on better by herself. She'd sent her husband, David, on a walk and told the twins to go and see Monty.

"But he won't be there yet," said Sel. "He said

he wouldn't be back till four o'clock."

"And there's nothing else to do there except mooch about," said Kate.

"Well, go and mooch then," said their mother.

Their caravan site was at Les Trembles, a small village near Le Touquet in the north of France. Monty's house, Le Bijou, was in Lefaux, about a mile from Les Trembles. The twins mooched up the road and then spent an hour mooching about the village. A little after four o'clock they went to Le Bijou. Slightly to their surprise, Monty wasn't there.

"Perhaps he's late," said Sel.

"Monty's never late," said Kate. "Think of him in the Rectory at home. Like clockwork."

This was true. Monty Goody was small, quick and always beautifully dressed. Although he was over seventy, his hair of tiny curls was jet black – their mother said it must be dyed. And he was always on time.

"When you've put on as many films and plays as me, darling," he would say, "you'll know you can't be late, darling." Monty often said "darling".

"Do you think something's *happened*?" said Sel, her eyes suddenly goggling.

"We'll have to go and look," said Kate.

Le Bijou was the last in a row of five small terraced houses. Their owners were all away on holiday, so no one noticed the twins strolling innocently round to the back of Monty's house.

3

"It looks to me as if you could get that larder window open," said Kate.

"I couldn't," said Sel.

"Not you, silly," said Kate. "Me."

Kate was efficient and neat like their mother, while Sel was absent-minded and clumsy like their father. Her hands would tremble and she would drop things or knock them over.

And in fact, when she squirmed and wriggled through the opened larder window, her foot caught a large glass jar and sent it crashing to the stone floor.

"Help!" cried Sel. "I've smashed one of Monty's expensive food things." She bent vaguely towards some round black lumps that had rolled about the pantry, giving off a faint, rather unpleasant smell.

"It doesn't matter," said Kate impatiently. "We'll clear it up later. Let's look around."

She seemed almost disappointed when they hurried through the little kitchen into the small, square living room and found nothing there.

"It's all just as usual," she said.

They stood looking round at Monty's pictures and books, and the little tables covered in knick-knacks and signed photographs of actors and actresses.

"It's very quiet," said Sel.

"Well, there's no one here," said Kate.

"No, I mean *sinisterly* quiet," said Sel, her fingers trembling.

"Oh, nonsense," said Kate.

4

Sel in these trembling moods made her feel uneasy. She would put on what Kate called her "goofy" look and say things were dangerous or sinister, and the maddening thing was that then Kate would find she felt they were too. She would try and ignore her feelings, but she didn't like it.

She led the way briskly upstairs and left Sel in Monty's elegant bedroom while she went through into the bathroom. She bent quickly and looked under the bath, then opened a small bottle of bath oil and sniffed it. "What are we looking for?" she wondered. "We know Monty's not here." She picked up a big soft sponge. "Clues," she thought.

"Have you ever noticed how pretty Monty's mirrors make you look?" called Sel from the bedroom. She was leaning against the end of Monty's bed, with one hand stretched out to the long looking-glass with its curly gold frame.

Kate went and stood beside her. Both twins were thin, with long fair hair pulled back under bands, snub noses surrounded by freckles and slightly sticking-out teeth. Identical to everyone else, to each other they looked completely different.

"See," said Sel. "We look really nice."

"Yes, we do," said Kate. "I mean, I always quite like how we look, but I expect Monty buys his mirrors specially."

Sel wandered over to the small dressing-table under one of the windows. "He buys everything specially," she said. "Look at all these tubs and tweezers and pots of cream. Honestly, Monty has far more make-up than Mum."

"That isn't very difficult," said Kate, thinking of her mother's two big jars containing the dandelion and spinach face pastes which Dad made for her. She had turned round to go back downstairs when she suddenly heard Sel give a sharp gasp and then whisper urgently, "*Kate . . . Kate . . .*"

She turned back. Her sister was standing at the dressing-table, holding something tightly in one hand and trembling all over. She had on the full goofy look.

"What is it? What's wrong?"

"It's Monty," said Sel. "Something terrible has happened to him. I can feel it. I can almost see him. He's in terrible trouble, Kate."

"No, he's not. You're imagining things again," said Kate, and she ran as fast as she could down the stairs. Yet as Sel had whispered "*Kate*", she had felt a stab of fear. Exactly the same stab of fear that had sent goose-flesh down her back when Sel had woken from her nightmare in the middle of the night.

"I'm *not* imagining it, Kate," said Sel, coming down agitatedly and almost tearfully into the room. "You know I sometimes feel things like that. And sometimes I'm right. Remember how I knew Millie would lose her calf?"

Kate came up and put an arm round her. "I'm sorry," she said. "I know. And I felt something odd

6

too. Anyway, what's that in your hand? Was that what made you feel odd?"

"Yes," said Sel. "But I don't know exactly what it is. It was among his tubes and tweezers."

She opened her hand and both girls looked at a small scrap of crinkled paper. On it was written, in Monty's tiny handwriting, "Thomé's tomb. Try the nose."

"Try the *nose*?" said Kate.

"Do you think Monty may have gone a bit mad?" said Sel.

"Perhaps," said Kate. "Maybe he's wandering about, not knowing who he is or something. But we must keep it. It might be a clue."

"No point in showing *them*," said Sel.

"No point at all," said Kate.

●

By the time they reached Les Trembles, the twins were quite certain something terrible had happened to Monty. They announced this together. Their parents reacted just as they had expected them to.

"I expect that old Citroën he hired has broken down," said their father, who was sitting on the steps of their caravan, trying to light his pipe. He was a big, calm, rather absent-minded man with a beard, and his pipe often gave him trouble. He smoked a special natural mixture which he made himself from dried nettles and dock leaves.

"Damn this thing," he said, puffing hard. "Those

old Citroëns often crack up like that." A sudden cloud of black smoke gushed from his pipe and the caravan filled with the pleasant smell of bonfire.

"Yes, but you don't understand," said Sel. "Monty *asked* us to be there at four o'clock. He's never not been somewhere when he said he would be."

"Besides," said Kate, "suppose he's gone mad?"

"*Mad*?" said their mother. "Whatever makes you think Monty's gone mad?"

"We have our reasons," said Sel.

"Now, hurry off and get your packing done and stop bothering about Monty," said Mrs Anderson. "I seem to remember he always said he might stay behind a day or two after we left and do some sightseeing. Anyway, David's ordered a taxi just in case."

Their father blew out a long cloud of sweet-smelling black smoke. "Probably unnecessary," he said. "I'm sure Monty will be here in the morning."

•

When they got up at 7 o'clock the next day, a thin mist was blowing about the campsite. Sel said she felt sick and could only manage to drink some tea. Kate had a bowl of cereal, followed by a boiled egg and croissants with cherry jam.

And there was still no Monty.

"You see," said Sel, as they loaded up the taxi. "We told you something was wrong."

"It is a little odd," said her mother. "I am rather

8

surprised he didn't telephone. I know he had the campsite number, because he booked us in from the Rectory."

No one spoke on the way to Le Touquet airport until Sel, whose mind was clearly on disasters again, suddenly said, "Isn't this a bit dangerous, Dad?" She pointed to the swirling mist, which had indeed thickened into a dense fog. "Suppose the pilot can't see out?"

"Not nowadays, darling," said her father, who was grinding up some more of his dock leaf and nettle tobacco. "Even the little Love Air jets have all the latest equipment."

Following the smartly dressed air hostess across the tarmac, they were almost upon the small Love Air jet when it suddenly loomed out of the fog. There were only six other passengers besides the Andersons and they all tramped up the steps and into the cabin. The twins managed to get two seats at the very back, which Sel had heard were the safest in a crash. Kate took the window seat.

"Not that I'll see much," she said.

"I certainly hope you will," said Sel. "I hope it will clear as soon as we take off. I expect England is in bright sunshine."

But it didn't clear. On the contrary, to Sel's nervous eyes the fog actually seemed to be getting thicker. Sure enough, after ten minutes in the air, there came an announcement.

"This is Flight-Lieutenant Crabbe, your captain, speaking. It seems that the fog over Kent is even thicker than over France, and Lydd Airport has had to close down temporarily. We have been diverted to Gatwick. I am sorry about this, but Love Air will provide free transport to Lydd."

"There you are, Kate," said Sel triumphantly, gripping her sister's arm. "I *told* Dad it would be dangerous. All my predictions are coming true."

Kate suddenly wondered, with a thrill of fear, if Sel's dream, the dream she had glimpsed, was perhaps about an aeroplane crash. But then Sel gripped Kate's arm again, even harder. "Kate! Kate!" she whispered. "I've had another terrible thought."

"What now?"

"You know the high luggage thing they had at Gatwick when Monty took us to Paris that time, the thing like a pyramid which went round and round and the luggage toppled out and came rolling down?"

"Yes," said Kate.

"Well," said Sel, her goofy look beginning, "suppose a dead body came rolling down? Wouldn't it be *awful*!"

Kate stared at her sister, who was staring back at her with her mouth open and her eyes goggling – and then she burst out laughing.

"Oh, *honestly*, Sel. Yes, it would be awful. And it would be awful if you opened the games cupboard at school and a dead Miss Johnson came tumbling out. Hundreds of things *could* be awful."

Nevertheless, with all Sel's imaginings, she was

10

relieved when they landed safely at Gatwick twenty minutes later.

A lot of other people must have been diverted as well, because there was a large crowd round their luggage stand. Kate and Sel pushed over to the far side to watch the cases coming in. There was something hypnotic about the way they appeared at the top of the tall, steadily turning pyramid, paused for a moment and then came rolling down.

Kate watched for a while and then became distracted by an extremely tall giant of a man with dark glasses who was standing opposite them. He was bossily pointing with a stick at various pieces of luggage while three men, two of them Chinese, scurried about and loaded them on to – she counted quickly – seven luggage trolleys.

And then suddenly, right in her ear, she heard a scream. It was Sel. With bulging eyes and shaking finger, she was pointing in front of her.

"Look, Kate," she cried. "*Look!*"

Kate looked – and saw one of the most terrifying sights of her life. Poised at the top of the pyramid was the body of a white-haired old man. He had been roughly trussed into a brown canvas bag, his head sticking out of the end. As she watched, the body trembled on the edge and, toppling forward, rolled down to join the conveyor belt. Kate watched, horrified, as it came gliding slowly towards them.

CHAPTER TWO

"Help, <u>please</u>"

Kate saw almost at once that it was, of course, not a body at all. Instead an exceptionally large leather golf-bag came wobbling past her on the conveyor belt. The "head" of the white-haired old man was simply a white canvas bag over the heads of the golf-clubs. Once again, for an instant, she had been inside her twin's head – but it was a typical Sel mistake.

Sel, meanwhile, had subsided on to their luggage trolley with a low moan. Kate knelt quickly and put an arm around her sister. "Are you all right, Sel?" she said.

Without opening her eyes, Sel whispered, "Did you *see* it, Kate?"

Kate shook her gently. "It's not what you think, Sel. It's not a body."

"Not a *body*?" said Sel more vigorously, opening and then shutting her eyes again. "But you saw it."

"It was a golf-bag," said Kate. "Look. You can

see it going round the end over there."

Sel looked, but could see only legs. She stood up and stared with Kate across to the far side of the luggage stand.

As they watched, three men pushed through the crowd, grabbed the golf-bag and lifted it on to a trolley. It was one of the seven, all piled high with cases and parcels, which belonged to the man Kate had already noticed. As the twins watched, he strode out towards the green "Nothing to Declare" channel of Customs. The three men hurried behind him with the trolleys.

"Well, whatever it is," said Sel, "there it goes with that sinister man. But I think it's very odd. It didn't just look like a body. It *felt* like one too."

"Yes, Sel," said Kate in a patient voice. "Anyway, there's your backpack. Quick. Mum and Dad are waiting."

Love Air had paid for a minibus to take all the Le Touquet passengers to Lydd. The fog had completely cleared by the time they got there and the small airport was bathed in late summer sun.

The Andersons collected their battered little Citroën Deux Chevaux from the car park and set off home. Their smallholding was close to the village of Redbrook, not far from Tenterden in Kent and only about half an hour from Lydd Airport. They were winding down the last lane before the farm when Kate said, "Oh, look. Someone's taken the Hall." In front of them three enormous, shiny, black Mercedes were blocking the road just before the Hall's gates.

"Just as well we're back then," said her father. "Geoff will be busy."

Tenterden Hall was a large, grand house outside the village, sometimes taken by very rich people. Geoff Dutton, who lived in the village, was the caretaker at the Hall and when there were no visitors he let the children play there. He also milked the Andersons' cow, Millie, if they went on holiday.

The huge cars now began to move slowly forward, turning into the gates, but the last one stopped in the entrance. All its windows were dark, so they were impossible to see into, but as the Andersons passed, the front passenger window slid open. A long arm was stuck out and dropped a cigar end, and then the window slid up and the car sped swiftly into the drive.

Sel turned to Kate, her eyes wide. "Did you see who it was?" she said.

Kate nodded, and then for some reason put her fingers to her lips: "Sssh!"

The man in the front of the car had been the tall, sinister-looking man they had seen at Gatwick Airport.

•

There was always a great deal to do when they came home after a holiday. Sylvia Anderson started to light the big wood-burning stove which she cooked on and which also heated any water not heated by the solar panels in the roof. This meant, in fact, that it heated most of the water. David Anderson hurried out to see to Millie. The twins took their backpacks up to their room to unpack.

"I do wish, David," their mother was saying to their father when they came down again, "I really do wish you could hang your nettles somewhere else." She hit one of the bunches of nettles and dock leaves strung above the stove crossly with a stick of kindling. "I've stung my forehead twice."

"I'm sorry, darling," said her husband, thumping a pail of Millie's golden milk on to the table. "I'll hang them higher up, but it's the only place they'll dry. By the way, I'm afraid all the batteries are flat."

"*Drat* it," said Mrs Anderson, hitting one of the bunches again. Electricity for their light was provided by a windmill on the roof which charged up a row of batteries. When these went flat, which was often, they had to use the candles made by Mr Anderson.

"Can we help, Mum?" asked Sel.

"Or could we go over to the Rectory?" suggested Kate hopefully.

"No, you can't, Kate. There's far too much to do. Yes, thank you, Sel. You can go round and put out some of your father's candles – and use lots. You know they don't give much light."

"What shall I do?" said Kate.

"You can help me with the animals," said her father.

"And then one of you can get some more soap from the store in the yard," said their mother. "There's none anywhere."

Their father also made the soap – strange, odourless, lard-coloured lumps from which it was impossible to get a lather but which he said were actually *good* for plants and animals. "It's a form of manure," he used to explain.

Sel and Kate were just starting out across the yard when Geoff Dutton's wife, Elizabeth, came wobbling through the gate on her rickety bicycle.

"Am I glad to see that you're all back," she panted, getting heavily off the bicycle and leaning it against the wall.

"We're quite glad to *be* back," said Kate.

"We prefer England," said Sel.

"Geoff has got new arrivals at the Hall," said Elizabeth, not listening to them in her plump, flustered way. "He was afraid he couldn't do Millie tonight. I was coming across to have a go meself."

"What are they like?" said Kate.

"I haven't seen them, Kate, but most *particular* they are. *Most* particular. They insisted Sheila and Albatross were let loose right away. Geoff had to come back and get them."

"That shows they must be *very* rich," said Sel.

Sheila and Albatross were two huge Alsatians put out to roam the grounds of the Hall and guard rich visitors. They seemed ferocious, but Kate and

Sel had known them since they were tiny puppies and to them the two dogs were still as gentle as anything.

"Have you heard from Monty?" asked Kate.

"I had a lovely postcard of lobsters early on," said Elizabeth, who cleaned and sometimes cooked at the Rectory. "But Mr Goody isn't back yet, though I expected him today."

"Are you sure, Elizabeth?" said Sel. "Today? Mum said she thought he was staying on in France a bit."

"Well, he didn't tell me then, Sel. Rectory's clean as a new pin for him. Mr Goody's particular too, *as* you know. But I must get on in and see your mum. I won't be able to come in Friday."

•

That night, as the twins were getting into their identical dark-blue pyjamas by the pale glimmer of six of Mr Anderson's candles, Kate said, "Now, let's discuss the situation."

"You mean Monty?"

"Yes. What do we know?"

Sel looked vaguely about their bedroom, goggling slightly. "What *do* we know?"

"Honestly, Sel," said Kate, a bit impatiently. "We know he was meant to meet us at Le Bijou and he didn't. He was meant to take us to the airport and he didn't. He was due back tonight and he isn't. And all that is very, *very* unlike Monty."

"And there are my feelings," said Sel.

Kate nearly made a comment and then didn't.

"So we think something is wrong," said Sel.

"And the grown-ups don't," said Kate.

"Grown-ups never notice how strange things are," said Sel.

"But we don't have any real clues, except that bit of paper you found."

Sel took one of the candles and went over to her chest of drawers. Kate heard her rummaging about.

"Dad's candles give out a sort of darkness," Sel said crossly. "Ah, wait a minute. Here it is."

She came back with the scrap of paper they'd taken from Le Bijou. Both girls looked at it. "Thomé's tomb. Try the nose."

"The nose," said Sel. "How's that going to help?"

"If we're going to be like detectives over this, we need more clues," said Kate. "Then it would fit in. Tomorrow we'll search the Rectory from top to bottom."

•

Monty Goody had partly retired from show business two years before in order to be near his niece, Sylvia. His house, the old Rectory, was about two miles from the Andersons' house on the other side of the village. David Anderson insisted that the whole family use bicycles whenever possible in order to reduce acid rain and the twins set out immediately after breakfast.

Monty agreed with their father about acid rain

and global warming and organic farming, but although he felt guilty, there were certain things he couldn't do without. The two girls heard the distant boom of central heating the moment they opened the door. A faint smell of expensive furniture polish hung in the air.

"Elizabeth's been busy," said Sel, sniffing as they hurried in. Kate looked round the hall: the marble statue of a naked boy, one of Monty's long, gold-framed looking-glasses, some oil paintings. It all looked exactly as usual.

"What shall we do?" she said uncertainly.

"Well, I think I may have a bath," said Sel.

She agreed with her father about global warming, and all the rest too, but she loved the way the water in the bathrooms in Monty's house came gurgling out boiling hot from the gleaming taps. She loved the lathery, foamy, bubbly soap and the huge bottle of scented bath oil.

"A bath!" said Kate crossly. "You can't have a bath now."

"Well, what then?"

"I don't know," said Kate. "It all looks so ordinary and the same. What did Inspector Morse do? Can you remember?"

"Sort of rushed about," said Sel. "Anyway, he had a lot of police to help him." There was a pause. "What we need," she went on, "is a body."

"Sel!"

"I don't mean Monty," said Sel. "Not necessarily. But Inspector Morse and Poirot and all the telly detectives have bodies. It makes it far easier."

Again, there was a silence. Sel began to feel impatient. Usually Kate was the more active and bossy of the twins, with Sel happy to drift about and follow her. But sometimes, for a while, there would be a change and she would get sick of being bossed, or if, as now, Kate couldn't make up her mind, Sel would find herself taking the lead.

"Look, Kate, we need to find either something odd or something which would tell us where Monty might be. A letter saying 'Meet you in Paris' or something. You look downstairs, especially his study. I'll do upstairs, especially his bedroom."

But the first place Sel looked was Monty's own bathroom, because she had never been in it before. She was not in the least surprised to find it was largely taken up by an enormous dressing-table with even more pots and tweezers and tubes and tiny brushes than at Le Bijou. Among them sat a small, red telephone. She picked up a pot of Lancôme foundation and idly rubbed a little on her cheek. It gave off a soft, fruity smell like boiled sweets. Sel leant forward and picked up a stick of Givenchy lip gloss.

A quarter of an hour later, she heard Kate calling her. "I'm in here," she shouted. "In Monty's bathroom."

Kate came in and then stopped, staring at her. "Sel, whatever have you been doing? Your *face*! *Honestly!*"

"I was looking for clues in his pots," said Sel

rather guiltily, "and sort of thought I'd try some. Come and look. It's amazing. Like a shop."

Despite herself, Kate leant over the table. "What are those? Eyelashes?"

"Yes," said Sel. "I was about to put them on."

"You can't," said Kate, herself putting back a blue Cardin eyeliner. "We can do this later. We're meant to be finding clues. Have you?"

"No," said Sel. "Have you?"

"Well, I may have. I was looking behind the pictures in his study to see if Monty was being bugged and you know that big painting of a horse, the one in his study?"

"Yes."

"Well, there's a safe behind it in the wall. If only we could find the key . . ."

"The funny thing is," said Sel slowly. "I may know where it is. I was coming down from our attic once and I think I saw Monty hiding something behind one of the pictures in his bedroom. He didn't see me, but he was definitely looking sort of secretive.'

They found it hanging behind the third picture they took down: a small steel key on a blue ribbon.

Running downstairs, the twins climbed on to his desk and Kate tried the key. It fitted and turned. She pulled the safe door open.

There was not much there: two large envelopes, one flat, the other fat; a paper bag of something; and another key. Kate picked up the key and together they read the label: "Le Bijou – spare".

"Spare for what, do you think?" said Sel.

"The door, I suppose," said Kate.

Sel reached in and took out the paper bag. Inside they found three small bundles, each done up in a net. They were wigs of tightly curled black hair. Sel unfurled one and put it on her head.

"They must be Monty's!" cried Kate. "Look in that mirror. It's just like his hair."

Sel looked. "You're right. Fancy Monty wearing a wig. But now I think about it, his hair was always almost too neat. I wonder why he kept them in the safe."

"Poor Monty. He didn't want anyone to know about it," said Kate. "Not even Elizabeth." She took the wig off Sel's head and looked inside. A small label said "Taiwan – Human Hair".

"Ugh," said Sel, shuddering. "Probably from a dead body."

"Nonsense," said Kate. "You're obsessed with bodies. Women there sell their hair for money."

Finally they got down the two envelopes. In the flat one there was a single Xeroxed sheet on which there was a diagram.

"This," said Kate in a serious voice, "is a real clue."

They looked at it in silence.

At last Sel said, "What's it of?"

"I think it must be a coal-mine," said Kate. "Look. 'Shaft 1' and 'Shaft 2'. Then 'Main gallery' and 'Side galleries', all leading to 'Face'. That must mean coal-face. Pity the bottom of the diagram was cut off. That would have said what it was."

"And where it was," said Sel. "Are there any coal-mines near Le Bijou?"

"I don't think so," said Kate. "But don't you remember Miss Johnson last term in geography? There are definitely coal-mines in Kent."

" 'Stage 1'," Sel read out, examining the diagram. "It must be the plan of a coal-mine when they'd just begun to dig it. And look how spindly and old-fashioned the writing is. Are there lots of *old* mines?"

"Probably," said Kate. "There must be. We'll get a copy of this and then we'll find out about all the coal-mines in Kent. Now, let's open the fat envelope."

The fat envelope was full of money – so much money that the twins gasped. There were ten plump wads of crisp new £50 notes. A strip of brown paper went round each wad and on each strip was written "10 x £50".

"Ten times £50 is £500," said Sel.

"Ten times £500 is £5000," said Kate. They looked at each other. "This could come in very handy in emergencies," said Kate.

"But how could we use it?" said Sel. "Imagine the shock if we went into Trevor's shop in the village with a £50 note."

"We'd have to launder it," said Kate.

"*Launder* it?" said Sel. "How would that help? It'd be daft. We might as well throw it away."

"You might as well be daft," said Kate. "Laundering money is quite different. It's what drug

23

smugglers do. They . . . they . . . Well, I don't actually know what they do, but what *we* would do is go to a post office where we're not known – like, say, at Appledore – and say, 'Our mum wondered if you could change this into fivers, please.' Then they'd give us ten old £5 notes and we'd use those."

"I see," said Sel. "Very clever. As long as we only need £50."

They put everything back in the safe except the diagram, which they kept out to copy. Then they hung the key on its blue ribbon behind the picture again.

Kate said, "You'd better go and take Monty's make-up off. You look a bit weird."

As they climbed on to their bikes again a bit later, Kate said, "All we can do now is wait."

"Poirot and Inspector Morse are always waiting," said Sel.

•

As it turned out, they didn't have to wait long. Four days later, Sylvia Anderson received an envelope from France. Inside was a short letter:

Dear Sylvia

Having a long extended holiday – several months. Tell Elizabeth not to come in after doing whatever she has to do. Love to all – especially Serena and Kate, my dear, dear girls. Please ask Geoff to jack up car in garage.

Love Monty

"There you are," said their mother. "A long holiday. So like Monty! And so nothing to worry about. He's fine. I must tell Elizabeth."

The twins were silent for a while. Then Sel said, "Why did he call me Serena? He knows perfectly well it's Selena."

"Too many big dinners," said their mother.

"The writing is very shaky," said Kate.

"Probably the same reason," said their mother.

"I think we won't go and stay with Sue and Jenny just yet," said Sel, looking at Kate.

"No," said Kate, "not just yet."

"It's up to you," said their mother. "They'll be very disappointed. You must write at once then, both of you."

Sue and Jenny Thompson were the twins' second cousins who lived in Norfolk. The Thompsons were organic farmers too, even more organic than the Andersons. They didn't even have a telephone, though it is true they sometimes used a neighbour's. There had been a vague arrangement that the twins would go and stay with them at the end of the holidays.

"We may go later, if . . ." said Sel, looking at Kate.

"If what? What are you two up to?" said their mother.

"Just if," said Kate, looking at Sel.

"Mum, could we take Monty's letter?" said Sel.

"I suppose so, if you like. But if you're going to your room at the Rectory, would you call in on

Elizabeth and Geoff and give them Monty's messages please."

●

"It's quite obvious something's wrong," said Kate a little later, when they were both sitting in their room at the top of Monty's house. It had two little attic windows, two small armchairs, a telly, a ring for cooking, bookshelves and a large green and red rug. It also had two bunk beds they used when they stayed the night. Elizabeth had come with them and turned off the boiler and already the radiator was getting cold, but they had turned on their two-bar electric fire.

"Yes," said Sel. "So obvious that of course grown-ups miss it. Serena indeed! He knows perfectly well it's Selena."

She stared at her wrong name and then turned the letter about and looked at it upside-down. Kate was examining the envelope.

"What's the postmark, Kate?" said Sel.

"I can't see. It looks like Sang."

"That means 'blood'," said Sel. But all at once her voice changed. "Kate, I've noticed something else. If you read the letter downwards, the first letters of each sentence make HELP."

Kate followed her sister's finger as Sel went on excitedly, "Having – H, Elizabeth – E, Love – L, Please – P. Help! That *proves* it."

"Not really," said Kate. "I agree, the letter is odd, but – well . . ."

"What do you mean, 'but – well'?" cried Sel. "Help! It's perfectly clear. Monty's saying 'Help!'"

"It's a coincidence," said Kate. "If you take all the *end* letters he's saying L-O-S-E. Lose."

"Yes, but you have to squiggle about," said Sel. "My HELP is straight and in capitals. And look, he's even underlined the 'please'. Help, <u>please</u>."

"Or you could take the S of 'several', the O of 'doing', the A of 'Serena' and the P of 'up' and get SOAP," said Kate, giggling.

"Oh, shut up," said Sel. "Just *shut up*."

She suddenly felt hurt and angry. The twins usually got on far better than most brothers or sisters: Kate led the way, Sel followed; Sel was dreamy, Kate was practical – and they both preferred it like that. But sometimes Kate went too far. And recently it had seemed to Sel that Kate kept on going too far. She'd disagreed about the golf-bag being a body; she'd stopped Sel having a bath; and now this . . . Everything Sel suggested, Kate pooh-poohed.

•

Back at home Sel carried on feeling upset all day. While Kate went to get the plan of the coal-mine copied, Sel typed out a letter to Sue and Jenny Thompson. But all the time Monty's letter lay beside her, saying, "Help, <u>please</u>." When she tried to convince Kate again, Kate just laughed and said, "Soap".

27

That night, as they were going to bed, Sel said, "Give me a hand with my duvet."

"Can't you do it yourself?" said Kate, who was brushing her hair.

"I can," said Sel, "but it's easier with two."

"All right," said Kate. She put down the brush and took the other end of Sel's duvet, but then she suddenly dropped it. "Sel," she said, "I've just remembered something very odd."

"Oh?" said Sel, trying not to show she was interested.

"Yes," said Kate. "You remember that golf-bag at Gatwick? Well, do you remember how it took three men to lift it on to the luggage trolley? You don't need three men to lift a golf-bag. I think something was inside it. I think perhaps it *was* a body after all."

"Do you?" said Sel in a careless voice. "Really? I don't." But in her mind's eye she saw the golf-bag rolling down the pyramid – and now, once again, it was the body of an old man.

"But *three men*, Sel!" cried Kate. "I think we should go to the Hall tonight and try to get in. It would be easy enough. You know, that broken pantry window."

"I'm certainly not going to do that," said Sel. "What's wrong with three men? Anyway, even if it was a body, there's no reason to think it was Monty's body. We can't just go chasing every body that turns up."

"But we agreed to follow clues. You said we should find odd things. This is odd."

"No, I didn't and no it isn't," said Sel. "Anyway, you don't agree with my things like HELP in the letter. Why should I agree with yours?"

"But this is *serious*," said Kate. "Please let's go."

"No," said Sel, and picked up her book.

But she went to sleep feeling unhappy. She hated rows with Kate, which in any case hardly ever happened. Besides which, she agreed with her. She'd known all along it wasn't just a golf-bag. In fact, before going to sleep she whispered, "Kate? You're not asleep, are you?", hoping that they could make it up. But Kate's steady, even breathing did not alter.

●

Sel was still unsure what to do, when she woke up. She lay on her back feeling unhappy and thinking: "After all, Kate *does* now agree with me. It was *me* who said the golf-bag was a body."

She was convinced she heard Kate stir. "Kate?" she said. "Kate, are you awake?" Silence. "Kate," she said rather more loudly. "I'm sorry about last night. I think you were right. Kate?" She sat up and looked over to Kate's bed.

But the bed was empty. Kate had gone.

CHAPTER THREE

Kidnap!

Kate had heard Sel whispering before blowing out her candle and had nearly answered. Then she thought, "No. If she doesn't want to come, I'll go alone."

She lay awake, listening to the noises of the house: the wind outside and the odd creakings. She heard her mother come upstairs. Her father riddled the stove and filled it with logs for the night. There was a click as he turned on the switch connecting the windmill on the roof to the batteries and at last she heard him putting one of his candles on the chest on the landing. For a while she could vaguely hear her parents murmuring together; then this stopped and once again there was just the occasional gentle creaking of the farmhouse at night and the sound of the wind.

Kate longed simply to go to sleep, but after waiting another ten minutes she got quietly out of bed. Luckily both the jeans and shirt she'd been wearing all day were black. She put them on and then very carefully eased open her clothes drawer, taking out her dark-blue high-necked jersey. She pulled it on, then tiptoed in her socks across to the door, stepped through and closed it gently behind her.

The light from her father's candle was so dim, it was actually hard to see. Kate felt her way along to the stairs and crept down, making deafening creaks. At the bottom she stopped and listened, but no one seemed to have woken up.

The kitchen was warm and not so dark, with a faint glow coming from the stove. Kate put on her gumboots and dark-green anorak, and took a torch from the line of them on the shelf beside the back door. What with windmills and home-made candles, the Andersons relied a good deal on torches.

Outside the wind was getting stronger and she could hear the swish of the windmill. The batteries would be charging up nicely. It was a cloudy night, with neither stars nor moon. Kate stood for a while, letting her eyes become accustomed to the darkness.

At last, beginning to wish Sel was with her, she moved across the yard and out of the gate. The Hall itself was a mile up the road, but the Hall park was only half a mile away. Kate hurried along the road, shining the torch just in front of her. Every now and again she aimed it to her left and at last saw the looming shape of the six-foot-high park wall.

Somewhere fairly near here a number of bricks had fallen out and it was possible to climb over. She moved slowly, shining her torch constantly until at last she saw the black holes in the smooth brick face. A few moments later she was standing in the darkness on the other side.

Now she really did wish Sel was with her. In fact, she wished she could climb back over the wall and be in bed again. No one would even know she'd been out. After all, what would she see at the Hall? Just the shape of a big square house with dark windows and everyone asleep. Also, it somehow seemed wrong, doing things on her own.

However, taking a deep breath she forced herself to leave the safety of the wall and set out into the night.

She didn't dare shine her torch in case it was seen, but there was a line of big beeches that led from the wall almost to the Hall. She decided it would be easiest to move along this from tree to tree.

She began to feel more and more frightened. She knew there were no monsters, yet she seemed to feel them all round her. She could hear the wind in the branches above her and it sounded like ghosts sighing. And perhaps there were men out from the Hall, prowling about with knives and guns. Twice Kate couldn't help flashing her torch, but each time there was nothing – only blackness.

And then, just as she was leaving the fourth of the big trees in the line, she suddenly did hear something. It was the drumming of hoofs, or the rapid thumping of several people running. Terrified, Kate drew back and crouched down behind the trunk of the beech. She wondered if the owner's heifers were in the park. Or the bull.

The hoofs or runners came nearer and Kate crouched lower; nearer and nearer, and then with a kerfuffle and a scatter and a rush they were round the tree and upon her – two jumping, smelly, whining, wagging, barking Alsatians.

"*Down*, Sheila. Down, Albatross," whispered Kate. "Sssh! Good dogs, don't bark. *Sssh! Sit.*"

She made the two huge dogs sit until they were quiet and then hugged them with relief. Had the barking been heard? She stood, an arm round each dog, and stared out into the blackness. She waited as the wind swished above, but nothing happened. "Come on," she whispered at last, "and *don't bark*."

Now she did not feel frightened at all. With Sheila and Albatross trotting beside her, she hurried along the line of beeches and ten minutes later the dark bulk of the Hall loomed up. Except, now that she was close, she could see it wasn't in fact completely dark. There was a faint glimmer of light from one of the downstairs rooms – probably, she thought, the library.

Kate ran across the lawn and up to the house where it was darkest. Keeping as close to the wall as she could, and still followed by the two Alsatians, she crept slowly along until she was directly underneath the window with the light. It was too high above her to look in, but a small, bushy bay tree grew up to the window-ledge and Kate was able to scramble into it.

She had been right. It was the library. The window was shut and the curtains drawn, but a small gap allowed her to see in. The tall man they had noticed at Gatwick was talking, but she couldn't see who he was talking to. Every now and then, though, he pointed to a large board on which was pinned some sort of diagram. Kate could see very little of this but it seemed to her that it looked very like the diagram she and Sel had found in Monty's safe.

It was impossible to hear what was being said. Kate heaved herself higher, trying to get close enough to put her ear against the window. But the added weight further up the bay tree was too much. It suddenly bent forward, striking the windowpane sharply and sending Kate slithering and sliding down to the ground.

She just had time to wriggle in against the wall and hide her face when she heard the window above her being flung open and a hoarse voice shouting, "Vot goes on? Who there? Stop!"

At once Sheila and Albatross, who had been sniffing quietly about in the flowerbeds, came galumphing up and stood below the window, barking.

"What the hell's going on, Heinz?" Another

voice, American this time, had joined the first.

"*I* know not vot," said the hoarse-voiced man. "Thees beeg dogs is jumping at vindow, I think. Ees too beeg, thees dogs, too beeg."

"Well, your shouting ain't helping any," said the American. "They probably saw the light between the curtains. Draw them tight. Shut the window. We've a lot to get through yet."

Kate lay absolutely still until her heart had stopped hammering and then, very carefully, she wriggled her way out from under the tree and walked quickly and quietly along the house away from the library. She'd decided to go all the way round the Hall once and then get back home to discuss things with Sel.

It wasn't until she was passing the old kitchen that she saw another light. Because the Hall was built into a small hill, the ground-floor rooms at the back seemed to be underground, like cellars. Their windows looked out into small areas, each one covered by a large iron grating.

It was coming up from one of these that Kate saw a faint glimmer. She crept forward and then, kneeling down, looked into the window below. The most terrible sight met her eyes.

Lying on a mattress, covered in two thin blankets, was Monty. The mattress was pressed up against a radiator and tied to this was a thick rope, the other ends of which disappeared under the blankets and were, presumably, attached to some unhappy bit of Monty. The saddest thing of all was that they had taken away his wig. Poor Monty had tied a knot at each corner of his handkerchief and was wearing it like a sort of hat.

Kate's first idea was to attract his attention, but what if, in his surprise, Monty alerted some guard? She wondered if she should run and get her father. But would he believe her? "Dad, wake up. Quick! I've just seen Monty tied to a radiator in the Hall . . ." Sel would believe her, but what could she and Sel do that she couldn't do by herself? And this was the moment, while those men were listening to the giant in the library.

Kate ran on round the back of the Hall until she got to the pantry with the broken windowpane. She longed to take either Sheila or Albatross with her but the window was too small, so she left them panting outside.

It was dark in the pantry except for a small red light which glowed on the dishwasher. Kate turned on her torch and swiftly went through the knife drawer, choosing a small but extremely sharp one. She opened the door into the kitchen corridor very, very slowly. It too was dark and silent. The kitchen and the door to the main part of the house were to her right. Kate slipped off her gumboots, left them inside the pantry and ran along the stone corridor.

She felt safer once she was through the door at the end and among the old kitchens. The air was dank, the stone floors cold, but she felt she could use the torch here, shading it with her hand.

She was fairly certain that Monty had been in the second of the old sculleries and, sure enough, as she came towards it she saw a rim of light under the door. Her heart beating more with excitement that she was about to release him than with fear, Kate now shone her torch directly at the door. To her delight she saw the men had left the key in the lock. She nearly called out, "Monty, wake up! I'm here!"

She was bending forward, knife in hand, and was about to turn the big key when she felt strong arms wind around her and lift her up. She heard a hoarse and by now familiar voice.

"Vot haff ve here? An intruder. Come, the Commander vill be *most* interested in zis!"

•

Sel's first thought when she saw Kate's empty bed was that her sister must have already gone down to breakfast. Usually they chatted while getting dressed and went down together. Did this mean they were still having a row?

But only her mother was in the kitchen.

"Where's Kate?" said Sel.

"Isn't she with you?" said Sylvia Anderson.

"No. And she wasn't in bed when I woke up," said Sel.

"Actually, I noticed her boots and her anorak weren't by the back door," said her mother. "I expect she's popped out to see Millie or something.

Could you bring the milk through from the pantry?"

Sel, however, pulled on her own boots and ran out of the door. There was no sign of Kate in Millie's shed, or in the field, where Millie herself peacefully munched. With sinking heart and already quite sure what had happened, Sel ran out to the farm's one big field, across which David Anderson was planting various hedges. No Kate.

When she got back, a pleasant smell of decaffeinated coffee filled the kitchen and her father was frying several of their chickens' eggs on the stove.

"Kate's vanished!" cried Sel, in her most dramatic voice.

"Vanished?" said her father, looking rather surprised. "Are you sure?"

"Yes," said Sel. "Quite sure. I can't find her anywhere."

"Sit down and have your eggs, darling," said her mother. "I'm sure Kate will turn up. She's gone for a walk or something."

"Kate doesn't go for walks," said Sel.

She sat slowly down at the table, thinking. If she told them, they probably wouldn't believe her; but if she didn't tell, no one would try and help Kate.

"Mum, Dad," she said. "I think Kate has been kidnapped by those men in the Hall."

"Good heavens!" said her father, advancing with

the frying-pan. "Why ever should they do that? One egg or two?"

"Kate and I had a sort of row," said Sel. "Kate said it was obvious Monty had been put in the golf-bag at Gatwick because it took three of the Hall men to lift it. She said she was going to search the Hall last night. I secretly agreed with her but refused to go because she'd been so beastly about my ideas. That was our row. When I woke up, she'd gone. Obviously, to the Hall."

"Why should anyone put Monty in a golf-bag?" said her father in an interested voice.

"I don't know," said Sel. "There's a lot we don't know yet." She realized how odd it all sounded.

"Darling, darling," said her mother. "You're both far too imaginative. You always were. We've had a *letter* from Monty. We *know* he's all right. If you had a row, I expect Kate's gone off to the Rectory or to one of your friends. I'll ring up after breakfast."

"She can't have gone to the Rectory," said Sel. "The key's still on the hook."

"Then Elizabeth lent her a key. Now eat up. I'll ring round in a minute."

Sel had no appetite and had to force down her egg and a piece of toast. Going up to brush her teeth, she heard her mother on the telephone in the sitting-room. "Sorry to bother you, Pat dear, but I suppose Kate isn't with you . . ."

When Sel came down again, her mother said, "It's certainly slightly odd. She doesn't seem to be with any of the obvious people. Come on, we'll go and see Elizabeth."

They found Elizabeth Dutton at the Rectory, doing a final clear-out and lock-up. But there was no sign of Kate. Sel ran up to their attic room, but nothing had changed. When she came down, Elizabeth was saying, ". . . such a worry always. Our Pete was gone a whole morning once – a fort in the wood. Kate'll be back, Mrs Anderson, never you fear."

But on the way home Sel could see her mother was beginning to worry. "I *know* she went to the Hall, Mum," she said. "You could just go and *look*."

"It might be worth asking them, David," Sylvia Anderson said to her husband when they got home. "They may have seen her or something."

Mr Anderson was crumbling a pile of crisp dock and nettle leaves into a bowl. "I will, I will," he said. "I'll finish this and go round."

"Can I come too?" said Sel.

"No, darling," said her mother. "I want you to go down to the village and see if Kate is with either the Pattons or the Huberts. They're not on the phone."

Sel knew Kate wouldn't be at the Pattons' or the Huberts', but it all took quite a long time to make sure. As usual, Sel had to explain which twin she was and, as usual, listen to the remarks people always made about twins. Mr Patton, who had retired, was very concerned.

"Would Mr Anderson like me to get some of the lads together and have a search on Blackberry Common?" he said.

"I don't know," said Sel.

When she got back she heard that her mother had rung the police and that DS Salter would be out immediately after lunch.

"What about the Hall, Dad?" she asked.

"I don't think Kate's there, or has been there," said her father. "Mr Commander couldn't have been more helpful. He's a big American chap and had me in. Place blazing with central heating, but never mind. They hadn't seen Kate but he promised to keep a careful eye open."

"But didn't you search?" cried Sel.

"Well, I couldn't just start barging about the house," said her father.

"Oh, *honestly*," said Sel, and she went angrily up to their room.

"She's bound to be upset," said her mother. "Poor Sel."

"Well, it *is* worrying," said David Anderson. "I'm upset too. It is most unlike Kate. I'm worried something may have happened." He went over to his wife and put his arms around her. "We've got to be very brave."

Sylvia Anderson didn't answer, but she pressed her face into her husband's coat to hide the tears that suddenly filled her eyes.

•

41

DS Salter was small, quick and efficient, with a little red moustache. He took statements from all three of them and made them feel that something official was happening. He was particularly interested to discover Sel and Kate were identical twins. "I'll lay on a photographer," he said.

"And will you go to the Hall?" said Sel.

"If your sister isn't back by this evening, we'll be calling on everyone in the neighbourhood," said DS Salter. "We'll be mounting a complete operation: dredging rivers, TV, posters – the lot."

While DS Salter was taking notes, Mr Patton turned up on his bicycle and repeated his suggestion of searching Blackberry Common. DS Salter thought it an excellent idea. "I'll put it to the chief inspector," he said.

Before he left, DS Salter told them that Chief Inspector Reynolds of Tenterden would be calling himself. "Inspector Reynolds takes these cases very seriously," he said. "Very seriously indeed. He has a young daughter of his own."

"When will he come?" said David Anderson.

"That I can't say," said DS Salter. "I'll give you a ring."

Chief Inspector Reynolds was going to come at 3.30, then at 4.30, then 5.30. Sel set out on her bike at 4.30, too restless to go on waiting around the house.

She went to the Hall. She would, in fact, have tried to get in, only a good deal seemed to be going on there. Twice, one of the big black cars drove smoothly out and twice it returned. Yet what if she were wrong? DS Salter – or David Samuel Salter, as for some reason Sel now thought of him – had said she could have set off for the Hall but been knocked down by a passing car. She could have been taken to a nearby hospital.

Chief Inspector Reynolds eventually arrived, with many apologies, at 7.30. He was a large, calm, comfortable man with several chins, and Sel immediately liked him. Her father asked him if he'd like some home-made beer.

"Could I have a mug of Horlicks?" asked Inspector Reynolds.

He said he'd like to see them one by one, and Sel joined him in the sitting room first. He was very easy to talk to. In fact, she told him everything.

"But I don't understand why you thought Mr Goody's letter was false."

"Not exactly false," said Sel. "I'll get the letter and show you."

Inspector Reynolds studied it. "Yes, I see. HELP," he said. "But what's this? Why have you drawn a line through here – SOAP?"

"Oh, that was just Kate making fun of me," said Sel. "That was really the start of our row."

But he was clearly more concerned by the diagrams. "I don't think it's a coal-mine," he said. "In fact, I think I've seen it somewhere before. But if your sister *thought* it was a mine, do you think she might set out on her own to explore? There are old mining works near Dover."

"Well, she *could*," said Sel. "But usually we do things together."

"Except you say she went to the Hall."

"Yes, but that was just to teach me a lesson, because we'd had our sort of row."

Inspector Reynolds stayed till nine o'clock. He refused to join them for supper but did finally accept a glass of David Anderson's beer, which he said was delicious.

Before he left, Sel said, "And you will go to the Hall again?"

"First thing I'll do tomorrow morning, Sel," said Inspector Reynolds.

●

Sel was very tired, yet she couldn't go to sleep. Lying in bed, listening to the wind and the murmer of her mother and father from the kitchen below, she realized that rather an odd thing was happening to her. She felt she was gradually turning into Kate. Or perhaps not quite that. What was happening was that parts of her which were like Kate, and which she normally didn't need to use or feel – like being brave or efficient – were suddenly becoming active.

She waited quite a long time after the grown-ups had come upstairs and then slipped out of bed. She put on her black jeans and shirt and then pulled open the clothes drawer and put on her dark-blue high-necked jersey.

She was just about to tiptoe down the stairs

when a voice said softly, "Is that you, Sel?"

It was her father. Sel stood still, her heart beating. At last she whispered "Yes."

A moment later he appeared in his pyjamas and led her back into her room. He sat her on his knee, gently stroking her hair.

"I thought you'd want to go and look for Kate, darling. But you can't go wandering out into the night like that. Think how terrible it would be if something happened to you."

"But I know she's there, Dad," said Sel. "I can feel her in the Hall. Why don't we both go? I know a way in."

"No, my sweetheart. Inspector Reynolds said he'd go to the Hall first thing. Leave it to him. It will all be clearer in the morning."

•

It was not clearer in the morning. When Inspector Reynolds arrived at the Hall he found it empty. A large envelope full of money also contained a note for Geoff Dutton: "We have had to return unexpectedly to America. Here is your rent." It was impossible to read the name at the bottom.

"Then they may have taken Kate to America!" cried Sel, when the inspector had finished. "What will you do?"

"There's not much I can do, I'm afraid," said Inspector Reynolds. "They haven't actually done anything wrong as far as we know. I can't arrest them. I've put out a description and an instruction to detain them for routine questioning. I've asked for any vehicle of theirs to be searched."

Now so much began to happen Sel scarcely had time to worry. Police and newspaper photographers took pictures of her in her black jeans and anorak to send out as photographs of Kate. Then all three of them drove out to Blackberry Common to help in the search. Nearly all the village was there and David Samuel Salter had brought thirty-five policemen. A TV crew filmed them for the local evening news as they moved in a line across the common.

After a quick lunch, David Samuel continued the search. Inspector Reynolds, who was personally leading the operation, took Sel in his car round all the local hospitals.

"We've sent out photographs," he said, "but it's far better if they see you and can see *exactly* what your sister is like. Might jog their memories."

However, no memories were jogged.

When Sel was dropped back in the morning, it was clear her mother had been crying. She said she'd been answering the telephone all afternoon.

"Newspapers, friends, television – everyone's been ringing up," she said.

It was a silent and unhappy evening. David Anderson broke his favourite pipe knocking out lumps of nettle and dock leaf ash. Then, suddenly, in the middle of supper, there came a muffled explosion from the yard.

"Help!" and "What's that?" cried Sel and her mother together, both jumping nervously.

"Now we're being blown up!" said Sel.

"Drat! And damn! And drat and damn," said David Anderson. "I knew I shouldn't have bottled that beer yet. I'm sorry. I'm afraid it's my beer bottles exploding. I don't know how long it will go on."

It went on at intervals throughout the night, twice waking Sel up. But she was very tired and instantly fell asleep again.

Towards morning she had an extraordinary and frightening dream. She was speeding just above the surface of the sea towards a huge, rusty, half-sunken wreck. She landed on the sloping deck and walked quickly down some steep metal stairs.

She found herself in a long, narrow corridor with cabin doors down one side. The middle cabin had a small window. Inside she could see Kate sitting on the floor, leaning against a radiator. Kate was crying. Sel was about to tap on the window and call out when she was seized roughly from behind and shaken.

So vivid and real was the dream that the shaking woke her. She even sat up to see who had done it. The room was empty, Kate's bed sad and neat next to her.

But far odder was the fact that she had recognized the half-sunken wreck. Obviously, Kate was a prisoner there. Just as obviously, no one would believe her if she told them. With a thrill of fear she realized that she would have to go and rescue Kate by herself.

CHAPTER FOUR

Into the Sunken Wreck

The year before, the Andersons had taken another caravan holiday, without Monty this time, in Scotland. It had been just outside the little village of Auchmithie, near Arbroath.

Here their father had made friends with one of the local fishermen, Jock MacFin. The twins had become friendly with his fifteen-year-old son, Jamie, who used to take them out in the small family dinghy with its outboard motor.

Then one day, Jack had suggested a proper trip in his fishing boat.

"Would ye no like to see the tanker wreck?" he asked in his soft Scottish voice. "'Tis a good old God-fearing sight, out there, so it is. Aye, and she'll no last the winter storms."

The wreck of a giant Chinese oil tanker lay three miles offshore, half submerged in the water. They had all chugged out with Jock and young Jamie and then slowly chugged round the great looming rusty hulk. Echoing booms and sudden gurglings and suckings had come from deep inside it as the sea surged in and out. Both Kate and Sel had found it frightening rather than grand.

Sel was quite sure it was this wreck that she had seen in her dream.

As she got dressed there was a dull thump-crash from the yard. The beer was still exploding. Then she heard the telephone ring twice. It rang again as she came into the kitchen. Her father answered it.

"It's police, photographers, newspapers," said her mother, looking white and drawn. "I suppose we have to do it all, but it's a great strain."

"Mum," said Sel. "I've been thinking. I've decided I would like to go and stay with Sue and Jenny after all."

"School doesn't start for two weeks," said her mother in a distracted voice.

"Good idea," said her father, coming back to the table. "This place is going to be hell for the next few days. I'll give Paddy Thompson's neighbour a ring after breakfast."

While all this was being arranged, Sel hurried over to the Rectory, but she had no sooner gone into the study than the telephone rang. Without thinking, she picked it up.

"It's Tenterden public library here," said a woman's voice. "Could I speak to Mr Goody?"

"He's not here," said Sel. She realized, hearing

his name, that in her fears about Kate she'd almost forgotten Monty.

"Well, I've sent him three reminders," said the voice fussily, "and no notice has been taken. He's six weeks overdue and fines are mounting."

"I'll tell him," said Sel. "*If* I ever see him again."

"I beg your pardon?"

"Nothing," said Sel.

She replaced the receiver and went upstairs to get the key to the safe. She realized she was going to have to plan very carefully. She replaced Monty's letter and the diagrams of the coal-mine in the safe and added the "Thomé's nose" bit of paper. Then she took out the envelope of money. How much would she need? She decided £1000 would be enough; also it wasn't too bulky. She also took a spare key to the Rectory from the board in Monty's kitchen.

When she got back she found that the Thompsons were expecting her the next day. David Anderson would drive her up to London in the morning and put her on the 12.30 from Liverpool Street to Norwich, where she would be met.

•

The rest of the day was spent helping with the search for Kate, which had now become very large indeed. Inspector Reynolds took her to three more hospitals, and then David Samuel took her to the railway station at Ashford and made her walk

51

about in the same clothes that Kate had been wearing when she disappeared.

"They have a poster and have been sent photographs," he said. "But to actually *see* your sister, as it were, might jog their memory." But once again, no memories were jogged. None of the people working in the station remembered seeing anyone like Sel.

David Samuel also told her that the three big black Mercedes had been seen once. An AA patrol man had spotted them heading for the M20 just before Ashford.

"So they could have been heading for Scotland," said Sel.

"Or Dover, or Heathrow, or Wales, or London. Anywhere," said David Samuel.

•

Sel and her father were to leave at 10.30 the next morning for Sel to catch the train to Norwich, so she packed before going to bed. She put the £1000 in its envelope at the bottom of her backpack, together with the spare Rectory key and a torch. On top of this she piled in enough clothes for both herself and Kate.

But one thing worried her. With all this television, her face – or rather their face, hers and Kate's – was going to be rather famous. To disguise it she put in their grey school hats, two hairslides they both sometimes used and two pairs of cheap dark glasses they'd bought in Les

Trembles. She wished she'd pinched some of Monty's lipstick.

•

The last of the beer bottles exploded loudly at 6.30 in the morning. As a result, the whole Anderson family got up early and Sel had ages to wait before they set off.

It was 12 o'clock when they arrived at Liverpool Street station and Sel's train was already at the platform. David Anderson bought her a ticket and then found her a seat.

"Now, darling," he said, taking out his wallet. "Let's see—"

"Don't give me anything, Dad," said Sel, immediately feeling guilty. "I've got masses of money."

"Masses?" said her father, looking rather surprised.

"Well, not exactly," said Sel hastily, "but I won't need much."

"Here's ten pounds," said her father. "You never know. And here's the telephone number of Sue and Jenny's neighbour in case they're not at Norwich. And you needn't worry about the train stopping. It goes Colchester, Ipswich – and Norwich is the last stop."

"I know," said Sel. "At least, I'd forgotten the stations, but I knew Norwich was the last one."

Her father stood on the platform, shifting from foot to foot.

"You needn't wait till the train goes," said Sel. "I'll be quite all right."

"Yes, well, I think I should get back to your mother," he said. "I'll just tell the guard to keep an eye on you."

"There's no need," said Sel. "I'll be fine."

"I'll tell him all the same," said her father, looking at the number of her seat and the carriage. "We don't want anything happening to you as well."

He picked her up and Sel felt his beard brush softly against her forehead as he hugged her. "Goodbye, darling," he said, and then she watched as he walked, with his big, rather clumsy stride, back up the platform. She saw him talking for some time to the guard, who was leaning out of the carriage at the back.

At last he turned away, waved goodbye to her and was gone.

"Something *may* happen to me," thought Sel. "I may be captured too." Yet she didn't feel guilty about her father, as she had over the money. Nor did she feel frightened. Ever since Kate had gone, she had felt strange: restless, nervous, a feeling that she had lost something important or forgotten something she had to remember. Now that she was actually going to look for Kate, she just felt excited.

Twenty minutes later the train glided gently out of the station. At once Sel began to worry about the guard. Once he didn't find her on the train, what would he do? Would he ring the police? But how would he describe her if he hadn't seen her? Perhaps . . . But in fact at that moment the guard, a small, sandy-faced man, stopped beside her.

"So you'll be the young person I'm to keep an eye on."

"It's very kind of you,' said Sel, "but I shall be quite all right."

"Naturally, your father was a bit worried."

"Is Colchester the first stop?" said Sel.

"Colchester? Your father said Norwich was your stop," said the guard.

"Oh, *silly* Dad," said Sel. "I'm going to stay with our friends, the Thompsons. They used to live in Norwich but they've just moved to Colchester. He keeps on making that mistake."

"Does he?" said the guard, looking a bit uncertain. "Well, he would naturally. He's bound to be in a bit of a state, what with your sister and all. I hope they find her."

"So Dad told you?"

"He did, and just as well. I'd have known you at once from the telly last night."

The station at Colchester was quite crowded, but the first thing Sel did was hurry with her backpack to the toilets. Here she took out her grey school hat, the hairslide and the sunglasses. She gathered her long fair hair into a bunch, gripped it with the slide and stuffed it under the hat. Then she put on the dark glasses. These were a bit odd but at least she looked slightly different.

By the time she'd finished, the ticket collector had vanished and no one took any notice of her as she left the station.

The first thing to do was to launder, or wash, or whatever it was Kate had said they had to do with the money.

The Midland bank was five minutes' walk from the station. Sel paused for a moment outside a shoe shop next to it and looked at herself in the plate-glass window. She smiled and said in her poshest voice, "My mother wondered if you could change this." She said it several times under her breath, each time feeling odder and odder. At last she rummaged in her backpack, took a £50 note from the envelope of Monty's money and put the dark glasses in her pocket.

In the bank, she stood on tiptoe and pushed the note into a sort of metal scoop thing. "Mum asked if you could give me some change for this."

"No problem," said the thin young man behind the glass. "How would she like it?"

"What do you mean?"

"Does she want notes – tenners, fivers – or coins?"

"Both," said Sel, feeling very hot and self-conscious.

The young man looked at her, then rapidly shuffled out various notes, filled a small plastic bag with coins, pushed everything into the scoop and tilted it towards her.

"Thanks," said Sel, putting the money into her pockets.

Outside the bank, she took a deep breath. So far, OK. Now the telephone.

There had been a row of telephones outside the station. Sel dialled the Thompsons' neighbour's number, asked him to get Sue or Jenny and said she'd ring back in ten minutes.

It was Sue who answered when she rang the second time.

"Oh, Sel, we're all so *sorry*. It's so *dreadful* about Kate."

"Yes," said Sel. "But the police have some clues."

"Clues?" cried Sue excitedly. "Oh, do tell me."

"I'd better not – on the telephone," said Sel. "But look, Sue, that's why I'm ringing. Dad and I are in London helping the police. I shan't be able to come for two days. Either Dad or I will give you a ring. Tell your mum."

It seemed to get easier and easier to lie. On the train back to London, and then again in the taxi she took to Euston, she said each time, "No, I'm not alone, exactly. My dad is meeting me at the other end."

The taxi cost £7.50. Sel gave the driver a £10 note and told him to keep the change.

"Thanks," he said. "But where's your dad? I thought you said he'd be waiting outside the station."

"No," said Sel. "*At* the station. *In* the station, on platform nine." The dark glasses were *very* dark and she couldn't really see the taxi driver's expression.

He watched her walk away into Euston. There was something odd about her, and it wasn't just the dark glasses. Had he seen her before somewhere? He wondered whether he ought to do something about it, but then he shrugged his shoulders and drove off into the traffic.

Sel found that the next train to Arbroath didn't leave for five hours. Now was the time to be really posh. She unpacked three more of Monty's £50 notes and went to one of the ticket counters.

"Mother's just buying some papers," she said. "Some glossies. She asked me to get the ticket. One and a half return to Arbroath, if you please."

"Sleepers?" said the rather disagreeable-looking woman selling the tickets.

Sel thought rapidly. She felt she might somehow look more suspicious alone in a sleeper. "Mother prefers the seats," she said.

The woman tapped at her machine. "Mother would have done better to book in advance," she said. "Ah – I do have two. Coming back weekday or weekend?"

"Tomorrow," said Sel.

"Weekend," said the woman.

"But Friday is a weekday," said Sel.

"Not to BR it isn't," said the woman.

There was a pause while she tapped angrily at her machine.

"Ectually," said Sel, taking off her dark glasses and then putting them on again. "*Ectually,*

58

mother and me are just going to the castle for a night," she said.

"What?" said the woman, not looking at her.

"Nothing," said Sel.

The tickets came to £114, which meant another lot of laundering had been done. Sel gave the unpleasant ticket woman a long, cold look through her dark glasses and then went off to "join mother".

She bought a hamburger, some soup-in-a-cup and three bars of chocolate. She went to the toilets to put her hair up again. She found some Cyril Bonhamy books in the newsagents and bought two she hadn't read, because they always made her laugh. At last, an hour before its departure, her train appeared. Oddly enough it was at platform nine.

Sel got a corner seat, took off her glasses and read one of the Cyril books, eating one of the bars of chocolate. The ticket collector came round.

"Are ye on your aine then?" he said in a soft Scottish voice.

"Not exactly," said Sel, keeping her head down. "Dad put me on here and Mum's meeting me at Arbroath."

"Och weel, that's fine then," said the collector. "We'll be arriving at 6.38."

"Thank you," said Sel.

She settled into her book again, but before long she found she was falling asleep. At 10.03 precisely the long train slid like a snake silently and

59

smoothly out of the station and set off north into the darkness.

•

Arbroath station in the early morning was cold and grey and soon empty. Sel managed to get a cup of tea and a rather hard ham sandwich. She didn't think she and Kate could have been on Scottish TV, so she let down her hair and put the dark glasses and hat back in the backpack.

"Are ye on your aine then?" said the taxi driver when she asked him to take her to Auchmithie.

"What if I am?" said Sel, who was sick of people asking her if she was on her own. "Anyway, you could practically say I was thirteen. *Actually*, if you're interested, my mum is waiting at Auchmithie."

"Och well then," said the taxi driver, "why didna ye say so?"

Sel could see the half-sunk tanker as the road turned down the little hill into the village. Even three miles out from the coast, it looked enormous; yet it was still not as large as she remembered. The back half seemed to have vanished. With a jolt of fear, Sel suddenly wondered if Kate had already sunk beneath the waves.

She found Jamie MacFin, the friend she and Kate had made the year before, playing as usual in the pool room on the front. He had grown about six inches and didn't seem in the least surprised to see her.

"Why, it's Kate or Sel," he said. "Which of yous two are you then?"

"Sel," said Sel, feeling rather shy in front of the young men lounging about.

"You canny tell them apart," said Jamie. "You'll ken the twins, Robbie?"

"Aye," said one of the youths, who had a cigarette hanging from his mouth.

"I didna know they still had folks in the caravans," said Jamie. "Is it a holiday you's on?"

"Yes, sort of," said Sel. "Jamie, could I show you something outside a minute?"

"Here, Robbie," said Jamie, "take over the game for me, will ye? Even you can hardly lose wi' a lead like yon. What is it then, Sel?"

Once outside, Sel said, "Jamie – Kate and me are in serious trouble. Will you help?"

"What's the two of yous done then?"

"It's not what we've done. It's being done to us. Look, could you take me out to the sunken tanker?"

"In the dinghy, do you mean?" said Jamie. "It's a tidy way – but aye, if I had to. Why?"

"I think Kate is being held prisoner there," said Sel.

"Get away wi' you," cried Jamie. "There's not a soul on her. What makes you think Kate's there?"

"I can't tell you," said Sel. "I will later, but not now."

"Why don't you go to the pol-lice?"

"I can't – *yet*," said Sel, in her most mysterious voice.

For some reason this seemed to impress Jamie. "Not even the pol-lice?" he repeated, beginning to look excited.

"Yes," said Sel. "I mean aye. We're relying on you. I'll pay you. I'll give you ten pounds."

"Och, I dinny want your money," said Jamie. "But it'll be a guid wee trip in the dinghy. Thank guidness it's a calm day."

•

As far as Sel was concerned, the sea, which looked fairly calm, was not calm at all. The little dinghy rocked and bucked, bounced and rolled; water splashed over the side and spray blew in her face. Although the coast grew more and more distant behind them, the tanker didn't seem to get any nearer.

Jamie sat at the back, the steering rod from the outboard motor in his hand. "Aye, it's a fair way," he shouted back when Sel asked how much longer.

But gradually the tanker began to loom larger and larger, until at last they chugged into the shelter of its great rusty bulk. Jamie steered up against it and brought the dinghy to a stop by the iron steps which ran down its side.

"She broke in half in the winter storms," said Jamie, looking up at the tanker, which seemed to sway over them. "She's right on the edge of a deep trench. They say she could slip over any time. I don't think you should try it, Sel."

"I know," said Sel. "But I've got to."

She looked back at Auchmithie. It seemed miles away, almost out of sight. They could have been in the middle of the North Sea. All at once there came a muffled, rumbling roar from inside the ship, as water surged and fell back in its sunken depths. It was a frightening noise.

"Some of the lads say she's haunted," said Jamie, looking at Sel with wide eyes. "Robbie says there's lights on her some nights."

Sel rummaged in her backpack and pulled out the torch. "If I'm not back in an hour," she said, "then you can get the police. I mean, you *must* get the police."

Jamie looked at his watch. "Right you are. At 12.15. Good luck."

The handrail of the metal stepway which slanted up the tanker had broken away in several places. Sel had to keep close to the rusty side. A gull swooped by, clearly interested in what she was doing so high up. But Sel had never been afraid of heights. Far more frightening to her were things down below – under beds, in cellars, underground, under the sea.

And, as she at last reached the top and climbed panting over the rail on to the deck, it was gurglings and rumblings in the depths of the great tilted and broken ship that frightened her. There were two bulkheads, each with a metal door leading below, one near her and one on the far side. Apart from these, the deck had been swept bare by storms. About a hundred yards away from her the ship ended abruptly in nothing. She could look out to open sea. This must be where it had broken in half.

It suddenly seemed ridiculous to expect anyone to be on this wreck. There was nothing but the echoing, dark and terrifying depths – the engine room and smashed oil tanks where black waters swirled, fish swam and bodies bumped about.

What had she done in her dream? Sel shut her eyes and tried to remember, but it had all become vague and got muddled up with what was happening now.

Somehow, she had to get down inside the ship. The door nearest her was held shut by a large rusty bolt. By working it up and down and then kicking it, Sel managed to force it back. The metal door pushed open.

A steep metal stairway led down into blackness. Turning on her torch, Sel took a deep breath and, trying to think of nothing, started down.

After about twenty steps, the stairs ended in a short passage and then continued down. If it hadn't been for her torch, it would have been pitch dark. Suddenly she heard again, but much clearer, the sound of water rushing in the depths. Sel, frightened now, went on down, her footsteps clattering and echoing. A further twenty steps and she was stopped by a metal door.

Running the beam from her torch over it, Sel saw that it was held top and bottom by large metal bolts. These were less stiff than the last one and she was able to force them back. She pushed the door – and at once she knew she had been right.

Ahead was a long corridor dimly lit by two single bulbs. So there were people on the ship after all, not ghosts. But, far more important, she recognized where she was. It was suddenly all quite clear. It was the same corridor as in her dream.

Doors led off along the right. Sel opened the first and flashed her torch into a cabin, but without pausing to look she ran along to the middle of the corridor. Here, as she expected, was a larger cabin with a very small window. Looking through, she saw a dim figure leaning against a radiator. Sel flashed her torch in and the figure looked up. It was Kate.

●

At first, when the torch flashed across her face and she saw Sel, Kate thought she was dreaming again. She had already twice dreamt about her sister, once so vividly that for a moment she'd thought they were together again.

The torch flashed a second time. Sel was beckoning to her, her mouth opening and shutting. Kate sprang to her feet and ran to the door.

"Kate! Kate! Are you all right?" She could just hear Sel, though not very well.

"Sort of – yes," said Kate.

"What?" shouted Sel.

"I'm OK, all right," said Kate, raising her voice. "But how did you know I was here? How did you get here?"

"I'll tell you properly later. I came straight down from the deck. Jamie MacFin is waiting for us with his boat. How can we get you out?"

Kate looked round the darkness of the cabin, knowing there was no way out. The window was far too small.

"Which end of the corridor did you come in?" she asked, pressing her mouth to the edge of the door.

"That end," said Sel, pointing to her right.

"Was the door bolted?"

"Yes."

"Is there anywhere nearby you could hide?" asked Kate.

"The other cabins don't seem to be locked."

"Listen, Sel. I do have a plan, sort of. In about ten minutes or a quarter of an hour one of my guards, a Chinese man, comes and takes me to the toilets. He comes through the other door at the opposite end of the corridor from you. My door opens inwards. I'll hide behind it, so he doesn't immediately see me. Then you . . ."

It was strange being a twin. Although she could only just hear Kate, Sel saw in her head what she was saying. When the guard opened Kate's door, Sel would leap out and shout. With any luck, thinking Kate had escaped, he would chase Sel.

Kate would have time to slip out and run to the door at the other end of the corridor, which also had a bolt. Sel, meanwhile, would escape through her door and bolt it. They would meet on deck.

Sel did not even wait to tell Kate she'd understood, but ran back down the corridor and into the cabin at the end. This door too opened inwards and Sel had to put her head very slightly outside in order to see properly.

Eight minutes passed. She thought she felt the big tanker shifting on the edge of its deep trench. She heard the deep rumbling sound of the waters below. Kate would be waiting tensely like her. Sel looked at her watch. She'd been away twenty-five minutes. If something didn't happen soon, Jamie would be gone.

And then, after exactly fifteen minutes, she saw the door at the far end of the corridor swing back and Kate's Chinese man appeared. He was carrying a large torch, which he swung to and fro as he walked down to Kate's cabin. He took out a key, turned it and was about to step through when Sel leapt into the corridor.

"Run, run as fast as you can, you won't catch me, I'm the gingerbread man," she shouted.

The guard stopped in astonishment, stared at her, darted his head in and out of Kate's cabin, then came charging up the corridor.

So fast did he come that Sel only just had time to get through the door and force the bolts shut before hearing a thud as he flung himself at it.

Four minutes later she arrived panting on the deck, to find it as empty and strange as when she'd left. A gull took off and glided out of sight towards the sea. There was no sign of Kate.

There was still no sign of her ten minutes later. Sel looked at her watch. Nine minutes to go before Jamie left. Should she go and tell him to wait? But if Kate appeared while she was away . . .

And then she had another of those odd twin feelings – partly a feeling, partly a picture in her head, partly a sudden anxiety about her sister. Kate was struggling, banging, trying to get out, shouting.

Sel suddenly found herself running across to the door on the opposite side of the deck. As she came up she heard faint hammering.

The bolt was even stiffer than hers had been, but by kicking and wrenching Sel finally forced it back. Kate almost tumbled out into the fresh air.

"Oh, thank goodness, Sel," she cried. "That horrible ship!"

"Quick," said Sel. "Jamie may have gone."

But as they came rattling down the steps, he was still there – just.

"Hi there, Kate," he said, steadying the boat as they jumped in. "Another three minutes and I was away haim."

"Be quick, Jamie," said Kate.

"Yes, be quick," said Sel.

The outboard motor started first pull and the little dinghy swung away from under the big ship.

They had just left the calm water in its shelter when there was a sudden *smack!* and a shower of splinters about a foot from Sel's hand; at the same time there was a sharp *crack!* from behind them.

"The bastards is shooting at us," yelled Jamie. "Get doon into the boat, the two of yous. Get *doon.*" He too ducked down and also turned the throttle up full.

The twins crouched in the bottom of the dinghy, which bucked and jumped as they bounced and zigzagged over the waves. They heard the *crack! crack! crack! crack!* of rifle fire behind them, but the boat wasn't hit again.

It was too noisy and rackety to talk, because Jamie kept the engine on full power, but when, after twenty-five minutes, they swung up against the Auchmithie quay again, he faced them both.

"This is something serious yous two got yeself into," he said. "We'd best go to the pol-lice about it right noo."

The twins looked at each other.

"We know it's serious," said Kate. "But that's the point. If we tell the police now, we'll scare the others off and we won't get the whole gang, or save Monty."

"We *will* go, but not yet," said Sel.

"And what am I going to say to my dad about this then?" said Jamie, pointing to the splintered gash on the dinghy. "He'll fair kill me when he sees all that."

Sel pulled the envelope of Monty's money from

the backpack and took out a £50 note. "Take this," she said. "You could say a tourist did it and paid you to get it mended."

"It doesn't look like a bullet hole," said Kate. "You could say he did it with an axe."

Jamie stared at the money. "Yous canny afford a fifty pun note," he said.

"It's not ours," said Sel. "We were given it by someone very rich who's on this case with us. We're *meant* to use it for this sort of thing."

"So it isny yourn?" said Jamie. "Aye, that makes a difference, aye." And he took the note and folded it carefully. "I can square Dad with this."

"We must get away from here," said Kate. "Is there a taxi, Jamie?"

"Auld Andy MacPherson does a bit of taxi-in' in the season when he's not fishing. I reckon he might – especially," added Jamie, "if you were to wave one of yon fifty pun notes under his nose."

Andy MacPherson would take them, but they would have to wait while he finished his cup of tea. His house was some way up the steep little village and it was possible to look out over the roofs to the distant tanker. Kate, who was staring back at her recent prison, suddenly took Jamie's arm and pointed. A motor launch had just swung out from behind the big ship and was speeding towards them.

"Is that boat coming from the tanker?" she asked nervously.

"Could be," said Jamie, shading his eyes. "Or

she could have come up the coast and we dinny see her till she came out from behind. There's no way of telling."

"I wish Mr MacPherson would hurry up," said Sel.

"I wouldna hurry him," said Jamie. "He'll be quicker if you leave him be."

Mr MacPherson seemed to be having a four-course, early afternoon meal. When he eventually appeared, the motor launch was three-quarters of the way to the Auchmithie quay.

But they had only just waved goodbye to Jamie and gone a little way up the hill outside the village in Mr MacPherson's extremely ancient car when Kate pointed to their left. The motor launch had altered direction and was now speeding along the coast in the same direction as them – towards Arbroath.

Sel raised her eyebrows at Kate. "Do you think—"

"I do," whispered Kate. "They could have a telescope or binoculars. It would have been easy to see us, and it's easy to see us now."

Sel leant forward. "I wonder," she said in her politest voice, "if it would be possible to go a tiny weeny bit faster, do you think, Mr MacPherson? The thing is, we said we'd meet our mother half an hour ago and she'll be getting worried."

"What's that you're saying?" said Mr Mac-Pherson.

The motor launch to their left seemed to be overtaking them.

Kate leant forward and repeated what Sel had said even more politely.

"Weel, we're doing twenty miles an hour the noo," said Mr MacPherson, "and we canny go faster than that. An' the traffic in Arbroath is awfiel bad at this time of day. We'll be there when we can."

At last they reached the station. Mr MacPherson took £10 and drove slowly away. The twins ran to the ticket office. The night express wasn't due for hours, but they could take the local train to Dundee now and pick up the express there.

The local train – three small carriages which were still almost empty – was already at platform four. They got into the front carriage and sat down opposite each other.

"Now," said Kate, with a great sigh of relief. "At last we're safe. You tell me everything and I'll tell you everything."

But as she spoke she saw Sel's face take on an expression of horror. She had raised her finger and was pointing. "Look, Kate," she whispered. "*Look!*"

Kate looked, and the sight was indeed horrifying. Two men were running towards them down the platform. They were the two Chinese men.

CHAPTER FIVE

Return to the Rectory

The twins stared at the two Chinese men in terror, then, as they disappeared into the first carriage, Kate scrambled off her seat.

"Quick, Sel. Get down."

They were only just in time. Sel had hardly pressed herself flat against the wall under the seat, when they heard pounding feet and saw legs run past. There was a short pause before they came running back.

"Kate," whispered Sel after they had passed, looking across between the seats to her sister. "Kate, my *backpack*!" She pointed up above her.

"*Sssh*!" whispered Kate.

Now more people were boarding the train. Legs passed to and fro along the passageway. A large couple came and sat heavily in Kate's and Sel's old seats. A man stamped out a cigarette about a foot from Sel's nose. The sliding doors hissed open and shut.

Five minutes. Ten minutes. Suddenly, with a slight jerk, the train began to move.

A little later, after some rather embarrassing moments with the middle-aged couple in their seats, the twins were together in the toilet, where they'd decided to spend the whole of the slow, stopping journey to Dundee.

"You can sit first," said Sel, "because of your ordeal. Now, tell me everything."

Kate did. After she had been grabbed in the Hall, she had been taken to see the giant in dark glasses they'd seen at Gatwick airport, and then again in the Mercedes. He was American. At first he seemed ready to take it as some little girl being naughty and had said things about taking her straight to her father. But then Kate had stupidly demanded to see Monty.

At once everything changed. The American ordered her to be locked up in a small room at the top of the house. Early next morning she was put in the back of one of the big black cars with her hands tied and driven to Scotland.

"So you didn't see Monty again?" asked Sel.

"No. But I did hear two of the men saying something about getting the old man back to the tunnel at once. And it sounded as if the tunnel was sort of near."

"That must mean the coal-mine," said Sel. "As soon as we get back we must go to all the coal-mines in Kent. And what about the wreck? Did you find out what was going on on the wreck?"

But all Kate had had time to notice before being locked into her cabin was a chart showing North Sea oil rigs. There was also a calendar with the date 15 September heavily ringed in red.

"So whatever they are up to is probably then," she said.

Sel calculated. "Five days," she said. "I wonder what it is. It must be important or they wouldn't have kidnapped you."

"Or tried to kill us," said Kate. "We could easily have been hit in Jamie's dinghy."

When Sel described the dream that had sent her off to Scotland, Kate said, "I think it was me who woke you up. That must have been the night I had an incredibly vivid dream I was back at home. I was in our room and I shook you and shook you and you were just waking up when the Chinese man came in with my disgusting breakfast."

Then, after a pause, Sel said, "What we had, Kate, were out-of-body experiences."

•

At Dundee the twins looked out carefully to make sure that the two Chinese men had not remained on the train, but there was no sign of them.

Kate and Sel had discussed going home but had decided they couldn't yet. If they were to be free to look for Monty they'd have to be on their own.

"We can ring them up later," said Kate.

There were still about six hours before the night express to Euston left but the man in Information said it would be standing on the platform an hour before that. Sel and Kate had a large meal of steak and chips and eggs, and then went shopping.

"The point is, Kate," said Sel, "that you were on television for several days. Or rather, *I* was on, being you. You're sort of famous in England. But that means I'm famous too. We've got to stop looking like we do and stop looking like each other."

They bought some black hair dye and a pair of scissors, and also some very weak spectacles from a chemist. Sel wanted to buy some clothes, but at first Kate wouldn't let her. "We must buy clothes in London," she said. "We don't want to look too Scottish, do we?"

"Why not?"

So they bought a kilt and a sporran for Sel, and some T-shirts, then Kate felt rather jealous of the kilt and bought a patterned sweater. They bought two small travelling suitcases and threw away Sel's backpack.

"I wonder if Dad is right when he says money isn't everything," said Kate, as they stood looking at some very high-heeled shoes in a shop window.

"I know," said Sel. "He could be wrong. Shall we buy those?"

They decided the shoes might draw attention to them and took a taxi back to Dundee station. Here Kate was rather cross to find Sel hadn't got them a sleeper.

"But why not?" she asked. "You did everything

else so well, all the laundering, et cetera, et cetera."
Kate had been very impressed by Sel's account of
rescuing her.

"I just felt . . . I thought . . . I wasn't sure if . . ."
said Sel. It was impossible to remember exactly
why she hadn't.

"Anyway," said Kate, "I can't just dye my hair
in the middle of the carriage, can I?"

"Well, there is the . . . but, yes, it would be a
relief not to have to be in the toilet for hours and
hours again," said Sel.

"I'm definitely getting a sleeper," said Kate, strid-
ing off towards the ticket office.

Sel followed her. How easy everything seemed
now they were together again. She felt a proper
person once more.

And Kate too, though she had been impressed
by all Sel's laundering and so on, hadn't been surprised. Locked in the Hall and then later in the
cabin, she'd found herself having odd, languid,
Sel-like fantasies. She had never had such a vivid
real dream as the one she'd had trying to shake
her twin awake. "Perhaps if we are forced apart,"
she thought, "we turn into each other."

The sleeper, which was first class, was wonderful. It had two large beds, the top one of which
folded down out of the wall, a carpet, a cupboard
and its own basin with four towels. Ravenous, the
twins sat on the lower bed and ate supper – Coke,
chocolates and chicken sandwiches.

Then, as the train gently flowed out of Dundee

station, promptly at 10 o'clock, they set to work. Kate cut Sel's hair carefully to about half-way down her ears. She threw the hair out of the window along with Sel's jeans.

"Embarrassing if it all came crashing in at a window further back down the train," said Sel.

Next, they dyed Kate's hair black. It took quite a long time, with a lot of splashing and mess, but in the end Kate's hair was quite definitely black.

"On the whole, I think my normal colour suits me best," she said.

Sel agreed.

Finally, the twins climbed into the beds, Kate on top. But, though they were both exhausted, neither of them slept well. They kept on waking up and listening to the rush of the train through the night, and every time she woke up, Kate thought for a moment she was still a prisoner on the tanker.

•

At Euston, by the light of day, the mess they'd made dyeing Kate's hair looked far worse. Somehow black had got all over the sheets as well as the towels. Kate said they must leave a £10 tip.

"But won't that arouse suspicion?" said Sel, in a worried voice. "Criminals always give themselves away by suddenly spending masses of money and raising their standard of living."

"No one knows our standard of living," said Kate. "Anyway, sleeping-car attendants are used to very rich people."

They left the £10 note on the bottom bed with a note saying "Sorry".

After tea and fried eggs and bacon at Euston station, the twins took a taxi to the nearest clothes shop.

"The thing is," said Kate, "we usually wear jeans and T-shirts and so on, so we've got to buy completely different things."

"Dainty things," said Sel. "Lacy, frilly, skirty things."

"We mustn't overdo it," said Kate. "We don't want to look ridiculous."

They found it very odd choosing different clothes. Ever since they could remember, their mother had bought them identical clothes. They bought a pleated red skirt for Kate and a dress for Sel, in which she said she did feel odd, so they bought her some dungarees and a new jersey to go with her kilt. Kate bought a velvet jacket. She also bought some jodhpurs, which she'd always wanted. They bought new shoes and rather smart leather boots. It had been decided that Sel would wear the spectacles. She said that in fact they weren't all that weak.

"It's rather like being under water," she said.

They were half-way to Charing Cross in their taxi when Sel, who was wearing her kilt, said, "We should really have done the rest of our changing in the shop."

"Yes," said Kate. "But we can use the toilets

again at Charing Cross. And we can look up trains there too."

"I suppose people on the run spend most of their lives in toilets," said Sel.

When they'd changed into their new clothes, which was rather fun, they threw away all their old clothes, had a hasty snack lunch and then looked up trains. They had decided to take a train to Maidstone, where there would be no danger of being recognized, and then a taxi to Monty's Rectory, arriving after dark.

"And we'd better call each other different names," said Sel. " 'Kate Anderson' is in enormous letters on all your posters."

"I'll be Martha," said Kate. "You can be Daisy."

"OK," said Sel.

They spent the afternoon buying supplies of food. Then they went to one of those expensive London cinemas where the seats are like armchairs. They took taxis everywhere.

"I see that the thing about being very rich," said Kate, "is how easy everything is."

"Yes," said Sel. "Poor Mum and Dad."

They had decided they must tell their parents as soon as possible that Kate was safe. And that she was with Sel, about whose disappearance they would soon learn. But if they said they were both still searching for Monty, the first thing the Andersons would do would be to come to the Rectory.

"We *could* go to them after all," said Sel, suddenly wanting to. "But as usual they might not believe anything."

"Also, it would be exciting to rescue Monty on our own," said Kate.

"Wherever he is," said Sel.

The 7.10 from Charing Cross arrived at Maidstone at 7.45, and at 8.30 their taxi dropped them at Monty's gates.

"Don't bother to drive in," said Kate. "Drop us here, please."

They got out. Sel, who could now see almost nothing, groped her way to the gate.

"How much?" said Kate.

"Like I said," said the fat young man who'd driven them, "twenty-five quid."

"Could I have the envelope, Daisy?" said Kate.

"What?" said Sel, who was feeling her way towards the catch on the gate.

"Could I *please* have the envelope Mum and Dad gave us with the money, *Daisy*," repeated Kate.

"Daisy?" said Sel. "Oh, *Daisy*." She fumbled about and held it out. "You'll have to come and get it, Martha," she said. "You know what my eyes are like in the dark."

Kate paid the £25 and waved goodbye as the taxi driver said, "See yer", and drove off into the dark. Sel took off her glasses, then they got out the torch and set off up the short drive.

The Rectory was cold and dark and somehow eerie in its emptiness. Though it couldn't really be seen from the road, they decided they would only use the torch, except in their room where they would turn on the lights. Here they hung two blankets on top of the curtains in the two windows.

They fried two eggs and two pieces of sliced bread on their electric ring. They were too tired even to watch telly, but before turning out the lights Kate counted the remainder of the money.

"Do you know, Sel," she said, "out of your £1000 we've got £564.20 left."

"It's amazing how much longer money lasts when you're rich," said Sel.

"Yes," said Kate. "We must tell Dad that too."

There was a short silence, then Sel said, "It's strange to think of them so close. Do you think we might go to them after all? That's what I want to do."

"So do I," said Kate. "Besides, what's tomorrow? It's the 11th of September. In four days whatever terrible thing is being planned will happen. Let's have a really *frantic* search for clues tomorrow and then decide."

•

But though they searched Monty's house all morning, they found no new clues. Or rather they discovered quite a lot of things that might have been clues or might not have been. It was impossible to tell.

Among his pile of old faxes they found one from

his Russian friend Zsa Zsa talking about a "CT film" he was to research on his holiday and several asking him to parties and meetings around the end of September.

"That proves he meant to come back," said Sel.

"Well, we knew that already," said Kate.

"Oh yes, so we did," said Sel.

They found a whole drawer full of share certificates, one bundle of which nearly seemed to be a clue. Among shares in ICI, M & G, the Channel Tunnel and Bass, they found some in Western Mining.

"Could this be something to do with it?" said Sel. "It must be about mines."

"It seems to be mines in Australia," said Kate, studying the share certificates. "We can't go to Australia."

"Why not?" said Sel. "We're so rich we can go anywhere."

But Kate was quite certain that if Monty was down a coal-mine it was in Kent. "Why would they bring him to the Hall," she said, "if they wanted him in Australia?" And while Sel cooked lunch she rang up the British Coal press office in London and made a list of all the coal-mines in Kent.

"I never knew there had been so much coal here," she said while they ate their baked beans in the attic room. "They mostly seem to be near Dover, but we couldn't possibly explore them all."

"I'd be very frightened of exploring even one," said Sel. "I hate going down things."

The twins decided that unless they found something really important and revealing in the afternoon, they'd go home that evening.

"They must believe us a *bit*," said Sel. "After all, you were kidnapped and you did see Monty."

Kate agreed, but she added, "All the same, it's a great pity we can't solve it all by ourselves. I really felt at one time we were proper detectives."

•

The breakthrough came at three o'clock. Kate was in the other half of the attic looking through old boxes.

Sel, who was meant to be searching Monty's bedroom, was actually trying out face creams in the bathroom and had become so absorbed that when the little red telephone suddenly rang, she picked up the receiver without thinking.

"Hello."

"Mr Goody, please," said a brisk woman's voice.

"Oh dear," said Sel. "I mean, he's not here. He's . . . that is . . . I'm his companion," Sel said, putting on a strange, grand voice. "Mrs Ambrose."

"This is Tenterden public library here," said the woman. She paused for a moment and then said rather oddly, "Mrs Ambrose. I'm doing a ring round about overdue books. Mr Goody is now nearly two months overdue."

"Oh dear," said Sel. "Mr Goody, that is Monty,

is usually so particular. What book would that be then?"

"*Books*," said the voice disapprovingly. "Mr Goody has three books out on the Channel Tunnel. One is a French one, obtained specially."

"Three? Goodness," said Sel. "Well, I'll see you get them back right away. Lovely weather we've been having." But the Tenterden library lady had already put down the receiver.

Sel stood staring at Monty's make-up, turning one of his tubes round and round in her fingers and having one of her strange feelings that something was about to bubble up in her head. Suddenly she ran out of the bathroom and up to the attic.

"Kate," she shouted. "Kate, I've had an idea."

Kate looked up from a large box of old newspaper clippings. "What?" she said.

"It's about Monty's library books. Don't you think it's a bit odd he should be interested in the Channel Tunnel?"

"Well, he's got Channel Tunnel shares," said Kate. "But a bit, if he is. How do you know he is?"

"He's taken three books out of the library on it. *Three!*"

"It certainly is a *bit* odd," said Kate.

The twins found one of the books, *Digging the Channel Tunnel*, on the floor beside Monty's study chair. The first two pages had large pictures of the tunnel works in England and France.

The moment she saw them, Kate pointed excitedly at the French works. "Look, Sel. The French tunnel comes out near Sangatte.'

"So what?"

"Wasn't that the name of the place where Monty put us on the miniature train?"

"I can't remember," said Sel.

"It was, I'm sure. And . . ." said Kate. Without finishing, she dashed from the room and was back a few moments later with the key to Monty's safe. She opened it and picked out all their clues. "There!" she said triumphantly, holding out the envelope which had contained Monty's letter. "See the postmark? It says 'Sang'. You said it meant 'blood' but it could have been Sangatte."

Three more pages and they were certain. There was a large picture of the old French workings with "Plan 4 by Thomas de Gammond – 1873" written underneath. It was identical to the diagram they'd found in the safe.

"So that's what they meant by 'tunnel'," said Kate.

"Yes," said Sel. "You see, it's all falling into place. That's what happens with detectives. Suddenly everything falls into place."

"And another thing that falls into place is this," said Kate, beginning to rummage among Monty's faxes. A moment later she held out Zsa Zsa's fax. "See – 'CT film' must mean Channel Tunnel film."

"What do we do now?" said Sel.

"We must find the other Channel Tunnel books,"

said Kate. "If this one made us see all these clues, the others may do even more."

But though they searched for two hours, there was no sign of the books. Eventually they gave up.

"He obviously took them to France with him, to Le Bijou," said Kate. "We must go there at once."

"True," said Sel. "We never thought of looking at his books. Shall we go alone?"

"Yes," said Kate. "But we'll ring Mum and Dad or the police before we go, to say we're all right and I'm safe."

They planned to ring after tea and order a taxi to take them to Dover the next day. After tea, there were further shocks. They were watching the local news when the announcer suddenly said, "And the police have reported that the second Anderson twin has disappeared." There were photographs of Sel, photographs of Kate, a video, appeals for help. Finally, a young policeman warned everyone to watch out for them.

The twins looked at each other. "Oh, dear," said Sel. "Poor Mum and Dad. The sooner we ring them, the better. We really ought to do it now."

"I know," said Kate, "but they'd all come right round here. We'll do it as soon as we've left tomorrow."

"In fact, we're really being *hunted*," said Sel, her eyes goggling. "That was my friend David Samuel Salter."

"It's a funny feeling, seeing yourself on telly,"

said Kate. "Actually, I thought we looked quite nice."

They decided it was too dangerous to call a taxi. Kate remembered a big lay-by with a café on the Ashford road, about three miles away, where Continental lorries often stopped. They would get there early and somehow get a lift.

They had the last eggs for supper and then packed their two new suitcases: all their new clothes, the torch, cheese, bread and a tin of sardines, and Kate's Swiss Army knife. They also put in all the clues, including the spare Bijou key and the Channel Tunnel book.

"How much money shall we take?" said Sel.

"Well, we've learned the more the better," said Kate. "It seems you can't have too much. And we may have to bribe."

They took another £1000 and all the French currency they could find – 3000 francs.

They had turned out the lights and were about to fall asleep when Kate said, "How did you know Monty had three books on the Channel Tunnel?"

"Tenterden library rang up," said Sel.

"You mean you answered the phone?" said Kate in a shocked voice.

"It's all right, I said I was Mrs Ambrose," said Sel.

It was a typical Sel reply and Kate found she suddenly couldn't be bothered to ask why being Mrs Ambrose made it all right to answer the telephone.

CHAPTER SIX

"The Companions of the Nose"

The twins reached the lay-by on the A28 to Ashford at 8.30 in the morning. There was a public call box beside the café and while Kate went and hid in the bushes round the back of the lay-by, Sel went in to ring David Samuel Salter. They had decided this would be easier than ringing their parents, though it was true, as Kate pointed out, that Sylvia and David Anderson wouldn't have been able to trace the call.

"Tenterden police station. How can I help?" It was a policewoman.

"Could I speak to David Samuel Salter," said Sel.

"I beg your pardon?"

"David Samuel Salter. Could I speak to him?"

"You mean DS Salter?"

"Yes."

"DS stands for detective sergeant," said the voice.

"Are you sure?" said Sel.

"Of course I'm sure," said the policewoman, beginning to sound rather impatient.

The conversation with DS Salter was very short.

"It's me, Sel," said Sel. "Listen, I've rescued Kate and we're both all right. Monty *was* kidnapped and we're going to find him."

"Hold on, hold on," said DS Salter. "Where are you speaking from?"

"A long way away," said Sel. "Tell Mum and Dad we're both quite all right and give them lots of love. Goodbye."

"Just a minute, Sel, hold on," said DS Salter.

"No," said Sel. "I won't. Otherwise you'll trace the call. Tell Mum and Dad everything is fine."

She put down the receiver and ran to join Kate. "I told him," she said. "I was very quick. His name isn't David Samuel after all."

Lorries rumbled in, the drivers went to the café and came out, the lorries rumbled away again. After half an hour a large lorry parked close to the twins' bushes.

"French," said Kate.

"How do you know?"

"Because it's got that 'F' on the back," whispered Kate.

"Could be Finnish," whispered Sel. "Or Flemish. Or—"

"It's French," Kate interrupted. "Everyone knows that. And I don't think he locked his door."

They waited till the driver had vanished into the café and then ran out to the lorry. Kate had been

90

right – it was unlocked. Inside, behind the long seat, was a bolted hatchway with a small window. Shining the torch through the glass, they saw masses of tightly packed furniture.

The bolt slipped back and they climbed through. "With any luck," said Kate, "he won't notice it's unbolted."

•

The next six hours were the most boring the twins had ever spent. By squeezing between table legs and past chairs and beds, they managed to burrow down to a sofa in the very middle of the lorry. And there they stayed with nothing to do except, at one o'clock, eat some of the bread and cheese. They dozed and woke up.

"Suppose he's not going to France at all, but Scotland or somewhere?" said Sel gloomily. "He could be *delivering* furniture."

"I know," said Kate. "Somehow I don't think so, though. I have a feeling he's going through the Channel Tunnel."

But soon after this, although the lorry had stopped, they could feel a sort of swaying feeling. They were at sea. Every half-hour Kate scrambled up through the furniture and looked out into the driver's cabin.

The swaying stopped, the lorry started up again and they felt it bumping and roaring as it left the ferry. They travelled a short distance and at last, at 4.30, they stopped.

Kate, who was crouching by the hatchway, called down. "Quick, Sel, he's not there. We must get out."

They found the hatch had been bolted again, but Kate took off her shoe and smashed the glass. She unbolted the hatch. They slipped through and moments later were running down the street.

They were still in Calais. Sangatte was only about four miles away, according to Tenterden library's Channel Tunnel book, but since they didn't know what they were looking for there they decided to go to Le Bijou first and get more clues.

"We'd better go via Trembles," said Kate, "so as not to arouse suspicion."

"It's not Trembles," said Sel, who spoke better French than Kate. "You have to say Trombla – *bla*. Trom*bla*. It's a dotty language!"

"Trom*bla* then," said Kate. "Can you do that 'Our mum said' bit in French?"

It took quite a long time to get the taxi driver to understand what they wanted. When he finally did, all he was interested in was money – 500 francs.

"It seems a great deal," said Sel.

"Well, we've *got* a great deal," said Kate.

•

It was nearly seven o'clock when they reached Les Trembles, and getting dark. The twins ran most of the way to Le Bijou and Kate took out the spare key. "It doesn't fit," she said after a moment. "It just goes round and round."

"Let's try that larder window again," said Sel.

This was still loose and Kate soon forced it open. They pushed their new cases through and scrambled in after them.

The little house was cold and dank and felt damp. Sel stood in the small kitchen. "Listen," she said.

"You mean how silent it is?" said Kate.

"Yes," said Sel. "I think houses sometimes miss their owners."

Kate took out the torch and they went through to the sitting-room. But here she suddenly turned on the light.

"Should we?" said Sel nervously.

"Well, Madame Dupont, or whatever she's called, who cleans for Monty here, knows we're his friends," said Kate. "We can say Mum and Dad are at Trembles again. She never seems to come here when Monty's away. Anyway, everything takes so long by torch. We've only got three days before the 15th of September."

"I suppose so," said Sel. "But let's at least draw the curtains."

They searched the whole of Le Bijou but there were no signs of any other Channel Tunnel books.

Suddenly Sel said, "You don't think that Bijou key might be another safe, do you?"

"It might be," said Kate. "Good idea."

"If it is, it will be behind a picture," said Sel.

Sure enough, they found the safe behind a picture of a young soldier on horseback in the sitting-room.

"Now," said Kate, climbing on to a chair and slipping in the key. "This is our last chance for clues."

"The key turned; the safe opened. Inside were two small books and a bag. Kate passed the bag down to Sel.

"It's wigs," said Sel. "Two more of Monty's wigs wrapped in a hairnet."

The books were the Channel Tunnel books. One seemed to be all about the digging machines; the other was in French – *La Vie de Thomé de Gammond.*

"Oh, dear," said Sel, turning the pages. "It will take me months to read this. Years."

But Kate was pointing excitedly at the top of each page. "Don't you see, Sel? It says Thomé. Thomé!"

"So?"

"Don't you remember?" Kate seized the envelope of clues and pulled out the scrap of paper Sel had found at Le Bijou two weeks before – "Thomé's tomb. Try the nose."

They found a rather smudged photograph of the great tunneller's tomb at the end of the book. Sel peered at it. "I can't *see* a nose," she said.

"Oh, there are bound to be noses somewhere," said Kate impatiently. "But look where it is."

Underneath the photograph was written, "Le

Tombeau de Thomé de Gammond – Sangatte".

The twins looked at each other. Then they said together, "Sangatte!"

•

The twins overslept.

"Quick, Sel, hurry," said Kate. "It's the 13th of September. Only two more days."

"The 13th?" said Sel anxiously. "Oh, dear."

Things kept on holding them up. No one seemed to understand Sel's French. The new suitcases were far heavier and harder to lug about than back-packs. The Lefaux taxi driver wasn't there. The one at Les Trembles, who remembered them well, said he would certainly take them to meet their mother at Sangatte but first he had to have a meal.

"It seems to me that taxi drivers eat more than normal human beings," said Sel.

They eventually left at 2.30.

They reached Sangatte at 4.30. The main square of the little town was much as they remembered it. Although the main area of the Channel Tunnel was a little way away at Coquelles, a few yellow-hatted tunnel workers were strolling about.

Before, they had really only noticed the minia-ture railway station and behind it the long wooden shed where the engine and carriages were stored at the end of the season. Now they hurried past these to the big grey church beyond.

Inside, the light was already growing dim from the large stained-glass windows. The twins' footsteps echoed and they found themselves whispering even though there didn't seem to be anyone there.

They found Thomé's tomb quite easily. It was at the back of the church and made of wood, with elaborate scrolls and decorations. The twins stared at it.

"Well, I can't see a single nose," said Sel at last.

"There must be," said Kate, "unless Monty really did go mad."

She rummaged in her case and pulled out the torch. Once again they both looked: ivy leaves, daisies and roses, lily buds and various other wooden blossoms, but it was true – no noses.

Sel said, "Let me look at the bit of paper again."

She spread it out under the torch. After a moment she said, "It *could* be 'rose'. Monty's handwriting is so tiny, it's hard to tell."

Once more they looked at the tomb, and now it did seem to both of them that the lowest rose looked, by the light of the torch, as if it had been polished. Kate reached out her hand and gave the rose a push. Nothing happened. She pulled it. Again, nothing. But when she twisted it, the rose turned like a knob. At the same time, they heard a faint click at their feet.

One of the big flagstones of the church floor had shifted about half an inch, leaving a dark crack along one edge. Kate knelt, put her fingers in the crack and pulled. Effortlessly, it slid back and simultaneously a light came on.

At their feet, a circular stairway led straight

down into the earth. After a pause, Sel said, "I suppose we have to go down that."

"Of course we do," said Kate. "Here, let's put our cases in that cubicle thing over there."

"It's where the priest hears confessions," said Sel.

Kate took out the torch and her Swiss Army knife, while Sel took the envelope of money and, just in case, the hairnet holding Monty's wig, one of which they'd packed. Then they stuffed the cases into the confessional, one on top of the other.

No sooner had they started down the staircase than the flagstone slid silently shut and the light went out.

"Help!" cried Sel. "We're trapped!"

"Sssh! No, we're not," said Kate. Pushing hard against the flagstone, she showed Sel that it would open again. "I'll use the torch. We're quite all right." But her voice was frightened.

The stairs wound down for what seemed like hours. As they got lower, Sel could feel that the concrete sides were becoming damp. At last they reached the bottom, only to find their way blocked by a metal door. It did not move when she pushed.

Kate shone her torch over it. Sel was hoping that perhaps this was it and they would have to return to the surface, when they noticed a small metal rose at the top right of the door.

"I'll try this," said Kate. She stood on tiptoe and turned it. The door swung open, at the same time bringing on lights in a tunnel beyond.

"Perhaps this is *the* tunnel," said Kate. "Monty may be here."

"Let's block the door open," said Sel, who was holding it. "We'll want to get out again." They found some short strips of metal rod and jammed the door with these.

The tunnel was low and dimly lit, and it sloped very gently downhill. It seemed to be made of rusty iron, though it had clearly been repaired quite recently in numerous places.

After they had run and walked for about twenty minutes, splashing through more and more puddles, and Kate and Sel agreed they had walked at least as far as from their house at home to the Hall, which was a mile, the tunnel began to open out and become higher and lighter.

And then suddenly they were in a spacious underground cavern. The walls were of curved new concrete, the lighting bright, and all along the sides and up to the ceiling were piled transparent plastic sacks. These in turn were filled with much smaller plastic bags.

"What is it?" said Sel, poking. "Sugar?"

"Probably dope," said Kate.

"*Could* be sugar," said Sel hopefully.

"Who on earth would store sugar down here?" said Kate. "No, I bet it's dope."

Sel, meanwhile, had run across the cavern. "There's a door here," she called back.

Partly concealed by one of the high mounds of sacks was a second metal door, this time held shut by three metal bolts. They pulled them easily back and then pulled the door open. Sel looked at Kate and Kate at Sel, then without speaking they hurried through.

Once again, a low tunnel stretched ahead, but this one was well lit, made of shiny steel and not very long. After fifty yards there was a small room. The twins took in another door, a telephone on the wall and a table. But directly opposite them was a radiator. Chained to it, slumped in an attitude of deep despair, was the unmistakable, bald-headed figure of Monty Goody.

•

"Monty!" cried Kate.

"Monty!" cried Sel.

The slumped figure stared and straightened. Monty turned his shiny bald head and a look of astonishment, even fear, spread across his face. "Is this a dream?" he said. He looked closely. "No, it isn't a dream," he said. "It's my dear girls, my dear, dear girls. My Selena and Kate. What on earth are you doing here? How did you find me? And what on earth have you both done to your hair? *Hair!* Oh *help!*" cried Monty, as he said this, suddenly remembering his baldness; and with another "Oh!" he put both hands on top of his head.

"Don't worry," said Sel. "We *like* you bald."

"We think you look younger," said Kate.

"Besides," said Sel, "look!" She pulled out the hairnet and showed Monty the wig.

"Darlings!" said Monty. "You are both darlings." He struggled to rise, but with a rattle of chains fell back against the radiator.

"Oh, dear," said Kate. "I've only got a knife. How are we to rescue you?"

"Nothing easier, darling," said Monty. "See that key on the hook beside the telephone? It's the one for my padlock. They hung it there so I could see it but not reach it. One of their fiendish tortures – one of many."

"What were the others?" asked Sel, interested.

"The others, darling?" cried Monty. "I'll tell you. But not now. You'll have set off the alarm. We haven't a moment to lose."

Kate unlocked the padlock and, led by Monty, who paused only long enough to put on his wig and cut the telephone wire with Kate's knife, they dashed back down the steel-lined tunnel to the underground cavern.

But they were already too late. As they came through the door, they heard the distant sound of shouting and clattering footsteps echoing from the other tunnel.

"Quick," said Kate. "We can get behind these sacks."

Scarcely had they crouched down when three men, all wearing the yellow hard hats of Channel Tunnel workers, came running into the cavern, crossed it and vanished down the steel tunnel.

Monty, his wig already slightly on one side,

hurried out and bolted the door shut. "That will slow them up," he said.

But the long days of imprisonment had weakened him. Their running soon slowed to a walk. It took twenty-five minutes to get to the circular staircase leading back up to the church, and Kate and Sel had to take it in turns to push a panting Monty.

In the church they were again nearly caught. It was by now quite dark. Monty had collapsed, panting and gasping, against one of the pillars. Suddenly, all the lights came on and once more they heard the clatter of running men.

"Quick," hissed Kate. "Get behind the pillar, Monty."

"I can't," moaned Monty.

"Get his legs, Sel," said Kate. Together they just managed to twist Monty roughly out of sight and hide behind the pillar themselves as three more hard-hatted men charged up. Luckily, they too were in such a hurry they didn't pause to look but disappeared rapidly down the staircase.

Monty had recovered enough to walk. Enough, even, to pause for a moment in front of a glass-fronted picture of Jesus and adjust his wig.

"I suppose you didn't manage to bring a little bottle of scalp adhesive?" he asked.

"No," said Kate. "Do be quick, Monty. Do all that later."

"Coming, dear," said Monty, giving his wig a quick pat.

It was not so dark outside. The few street lights were just coming on, but the streets themselves were almost empty.

"Freedom!" cried Monty. "You've no idea what it means. We must get a taxi."

As they hurried across the churchyard a lorry stopped on the far side of the square and a number of yellow-hatted men leapt from its back.

"Oh, dear," said Monty, stopping abruptly.

"What's wrong?" said the twins, speaking together.

"I don't like that at *all*," said Monty, pointing at the yellow-hatted men, who were now spreading round the square at the run. "What are Channel Tunnel workmen doing in Sangatte at this hour? This means trouble."

"Well, we can't stay here," said Kate. "Let's get behind the miniature railway shed."

It was Sel who was first across the low wall, and it was Sel who noticed the two loose boards as they edged along behind the wooden shed.

"Hey, Kate," she called in a low voice. "Look at this." Kate joined her and together they pulled at the boards. Monty joined them. With a sudden crack, they swung out from the wall. Monty, puffing again and holding his wig, crawled through, followed by the twins, who pulled the two planks back shut behind them.

As their eyes grew accustomed to the near darkness, they began to see the outline of the carriages and engine of the Sangatte miniature railway. At the back, a pile of coal reached nearly ten feet up the wall of the shed, where there was a small window.

"Well, at least we're safe here," said Sel. "Now we just have to wait till they go away."

"Sssh, darling," whispered Monty. "Those fiends won't go away. They'll search every corner till they find us." And at that moment, as if the men had heard what he said, there came a loud rattling and shaking from the tall double doors. Fortunately, they were firmly locked and did not give way. The rattling stopped.

"Alack! Alack!" said Monty, in a soft but theatrical voice. "It will be crowbars next and sledge-hammers."

They all three stood nervously listening. Then Kate said, "Well, we must escape."

She and Sel looked at each other. Sel said, "Are you thinking what I'm thinking?"

Kate nodded.

She turned on the torch and she and Sel threaded their way through the carriages till they reached the miniature steam engine. The little tender, full of coal, was attached to it. Kate flashed the torch over the controls.

"Can you remember how it worked?" Sel said. All she could remember herself was how frightened she'd been when they'd been on the little engine before.

"Sort of," said Kate. "That was the brake, and

103

you shoved that lever to make it go faster or slower. Dead easy."

"Yes," said Sel, who hadn't the faintest idea what any of the levers did.

Monty still had his lighter – "The only thing they left me, darling." There was wood stacked beside the coal. Soon a small fire had begun inside the engine. They piled on coal and it grew larger and larger. Smoke began to rise towards the roof of the shed.

Kate and Sel sat inside the tiny cabin of the engine and added lump after lump of coal. Monty leant against the outside and in a low voice told them what had happened to him.

It began the day he had brought them to have a ride on the Sangatte miniature railway. He had been sitting in a café thinking about his Channel Tunnel film. It was to be a disaster movie of sabotage and blowing things up. All at once, the men at the next table began to talk loudly in Russian, no doubt supposing no one understood.

"A language I know well, of course, thanks to Zsa Zsa," said Monty. "She taught it to me."

They were clearly criminals of some sort, yet to his surprise they seemed to be talking about the roses on Thomé de Gammond's tomb. Monty knew the name because de Gammond had nearly dug one of the first Channel tunnels.

When the men had gone, Monty had strolled to the church and, like Sel and Kate, noticed the odd polished rose, turned it and seen the staircase. But by then it it was time to collect the twins off the miniature railway.

"We noticed you looked a bit excited," said Kate, throwing more coal on to the fire.

"We commented on it," said Sel.

The next day, setting out early in order to be back in time for tea, as he'd promised, Monty had driven to Sangatte again. He had descended the stairs and found the cavern and the sacks. He, however, had opened one of the sacks.

"And, of course," said Monty, coughing and rubbing his eyes, which had begun to water, "you can guess what I found."

"Yes," said Sel. "Sugar."

"Heroin," said Monty. He coughed violently again, and again wiped his eyes. "Heroin and cocaine."

But worse was to follow. Creeping down the smaller steel tunnel, he had almost reached the room at the end, when once again he had heard Russian. There were three men there, explaining to a fourth exactly how the heroin was to be passed into the Channel Tunnel and across to accomplices on board the trains.

"Unfortunately," said Monty, "some of that dangerous powder must have got up my nose, because I suddenly sneezed."

He had been tied up and chained to the radiator, his watch taken, his pen, his wallet. "Then," said Monty, "the tortures began. They pulled off my wig. They said they wouldn't give it back unless I told them of a safe hide-out in the south of England. I had a brainwave – the Hall at Redbrook, I thought I could escape, or somehow attract attention." But the next day he had been given an injection of some powerful drug.

"I must have been unconscious for hours," said Monty. "I came to, to discover that I seemed to have been laid out on the middle seat of a car. They had also stuffed me into an enormous golf-bag. I couldn't see. I could hardly breathe. The golf-bag, with me and all the golf-clubs, was extremely crowded."

But he could hear. It gradually became clear that the Russian drug gang had teamed up with one of the Chinese Triad terrorist groups. Using the drug money, they had bought six Russian mini-subs. They planned to take these and stick limpet mines to all the North Sea oil rigs. They would then demand vast amounts of money in return for not blowing up the rigs.

"The terrible thing is," said Monty, "I didn't learn when they would do this or from where."

"But *we* know," said the twins excitedly. Quickly they told him of their own discoveries.

By now the shed was so full of smoke that all three of them were choking, their eyes streaming.

"I *think* it's ready," said Kate, looking at one of the two dials.

"It is sort of bubbling," said Sel, coughing and wiping her eyes.

"We must go *anyway*, darling," gasped Monty.

"We'll suffocate if we stay here any longer."

He reached out a hand and began to clamber up into the cabin. Sel climbed up on to the coal to make room for him.

But at that moment there came a crash from the double doors. One crash and then another. And this time splinters of wood showered into the shed. The gang was smashing their way in.

"What shall we do?" whispered Sel, and then she coughed and choked again.

"*Do*, darling?" said Monty in a muffled voice, now breathing and speaking through his handkerchief. "We let 'em get the doors open for us – quicker the better."

Crash! Crash! Crash! Crash! Chunks of wood were now flying; gaps and holes appeared in the wood. Crash! Crash! Crash! Suddenly the tall double doors of the train shed swept open. At the same moment Kate let off the brake and flung the speed lever full ahead.

A huge billowing cloud of coal smoke swept over the men outside. For a moment they could see nothing, then, with a rapid chuff-chuff-chuff-chuff like a train in a cartoon, the engine of the Sangatte miniature railway and its coal tender appeared slowly out of the swirls.

Slowly, but with ever increasing speed.

Monty shovelled coal on to the fire; Kate pushed hard on the speed lever; Sel sat on the coal and pushed it towards Monty with her feet.

There was a moment of astonishment and then

shouts of anger from the drug gang. Men came running from all sides. As they drew close, Sel hurled lumps of coal at them.

"Faster, Kate," she shouted. "Faster."

"I *am*," Kate shouted back. As one man caught them up, Monty swung his shovel, caught him a violent blow on his tin hat and sent him staggering back.

Without its carriages, the engine picked up speed more and more rapidly. It was now moving faster than the men could run. Suddenly there came a sound familiar to the twins – the crack of rifle fire.

"Get down, Sel," cried Kate, slamming shut the fire door, and all three crammed down together as the engine picked up speed. Crack! Ping! Crack! Ping! Crack! Ping! Three times they were hit, and once a piece of coal shattered on the tender, behind Sel's head. Then the engine swept over the road, away from the square, passed the last houses and so out on to the line beside the sea.

The ride, at first, was one of the most thrilling things the twins had ever done. There was a full moon that night and they could see the black shadow of their smoke streaming back on the grass bank beside the track. To the right, the waves rolled and broke white and foamy upon the shore.

Instead of being frightened, Sel became more and more excited. "Faster, Kate," she yelled, shoving more and more coal down to Monty. "Faster, faster, *faster*!"

And, as Monty threw coal into the fire, faster

and faster they went: 50, 60 and, at last, 70 kilometres an hour. As the line curved past Escalles the engine was rocking dangerously.

"*Faster!*" shouted Sel.

Kate pulled on the whistle and a tremendous "Wheeeee!" echoed through the night.

"I can't go on," Monty shouted suddenly, half collapsing.

"We'll swap," shouted Sel. She slithered down into the cabin and Monty clambered gasping up on to the coal tender. But no sooner was he there than there was a piercing scream.

"My wig!" shrieked Monty. "Stop! Stop! My wig!"

Sel looked back. Monty's wig had vanished behind them. Kate didn't even touch the brakes. Instead, she turned down a small switch she'd just noticed beside the whistle rope.

At once, two powerful headlights flung a broad beam of light ahead of the engine.

"Look, Sel," shouted Kate. "It's like your dream."

Sel looked and indeed it was. They seemed to be speeding along, almost flying along a great carpet of light. Remembering her dream, which had really been a nightmare, she turned and looked back. And at once it became a nightmare again.

About a mile behind them she could see five or six round lights like eyes swiftly following them down the railway line. Pursuit! Just as she had dreamt, the drug gang were chasing after them.

Too frightened to speak, she touched Kate's shoulder and pointed.

Now the shovelling became a frenzy. Kate found a clip that held the speed lever full ahead. She joined Sel in hurling coal into the fire. It roared and flared: 75, 76, 77, 78, 79, 80! The sides of the boiler began to glow red-hot. The engine swayed and shuddered. But still the round eyes behind them steadily gained.

"It's no good," shouted Kate. "We'll just blow up. Sel, you remember there were two stations? I think that glow in the sky must be the first one. I'm going to try and stop the train. We'll jump out, then I'll jam on the speed lever again."

The glow ahead grew rapidly nearer. Houses and streets flashed by – then there was the station of Wissant. Kate pulled back the speed lever and pulled hard on the brake. At once, as the brakes locked, the twins were flung forward and Monty came tumbling down in a shower of coal on top of them. With a terrifying screaming of brakes and wheels and showers of sparks, they slid right through Wissant station and stopped about fifty yards beyond it.

Monty and Sel scrambled out of the train, Kate let off the brake, slipped the speed lever full ahead again and jumped out on to the track. Then all three crouched down and watched the engine slowly, slowly start forward. Slowly, then gradually faster, faster, until at last it vanished round a corner into the moonlit night.

Four minutes later, six motorcycles roared and bounced past them. The front rider had a Kalashnikov, which he was firing as he drove. In a few seconds they too had gone.

CHAPTER SEVEN

Home Again

There is not a great deal left to tell. The twins helped Monty back on to the platform of Wissant miniature railway station. He was shaking and trembling, but soon recovered when Sel suggested he wore the hairnet bag which had held his wig.

Monty peered at himself by the light of Kate's torch in the glass window of the ticket kiosk.

"Well, darling, it certainly gives the *impression* of hair," he said in a pleased voice.

"You look very nice," said Kate.

"Very *fetching*," said Sel, using one of Monty's favourite words.

Shortly after this they were in Wissant police station. Monty explained rapidly to the chief of the gendarmerie what had been happening. Two hours later, three lorryloads of riot police roared out of Calais, surrounded the church in Sangatte and, following the instructions given by Monty, descended into the tunnel. It was one of the largest amounts of heroin ever seized – 10 million pounds' worth. Ten of the gang were caught, and five more caught later trying to escape on the Paris motorway.

While this was going on, Monty and the twins had been driven at a more leisurely pace from Wissant to Sangatte. When the raid had been completed, Kate and Sel recovered their cases from the confession box. Kate gave Monty back the key to the Le Bijou safe and Sel gave him his envelope of money.

"I'm afraid we had to spend rather a lot," she said, after explaining how they'd raided his safe in the Rectory.

"Darling," said Monty, giving a pat to his hairnet, "as far as I'm concerned, you could have spent the lot."

It was now nearly midnight. They were all hungry and tired, but there were now only twenty-four hours to go before the deadline of 15 September. While they ate some cold chicken stuffed with pâté and Monty drank a bottle of wine, complicated telephone calls went on.

The chief of the Calais police said he would do anything for them. Thanks to him, Monty was soon speaking to the beautiful French Minister of the Interior, Madame de Panache. And thanks to Madame de Panache, he was soon speaking to the Admiral of the Fleet and the head of MI6 in London.

It seemed that British Intelligence had heard rumours of terrorist activity in the North Sea some weeks before. All they had lacked were the details.

"Look, Goody," said the Admiral of the Fleet briskly, "I want all three of you flown back here immediately. To Dundee. I'll get one of our Polaris subs down to Arbroath with a fleet of anti-mini-sub mini-subs. Is that clear?"

"Yes, sir," said Monty nervously, feeling that he had somehow joined the navy.

More calls flashed between the lovely Madame de Panache and the chief of Calais's police, and soon Monty and the twins were speeding through the night towards the airport at Le Touquet in a convoy of big police Citroëns with wailing sirens and flashing lights.

Kate and Sel, however, fell fast asleep. They were asleep when Monty asked the convoy to turn aside at Lefaux and stop at Le Bijou for him to collect a new wig and some scalp adhesive. He decided not to wake them while he made a quick phone call from there to the Andersons.

The twins woke briefly while they transferred into a French Mirage X8 jet, but, tucked warmly in by the kindly French pilot, they fell asleep again almost at once. They didn't wake until the plane landed at Dundee airport early the next morning.

Here, over a breakfast of bacon and eggs and baked beans, Kate answered the questions of a young naval captain called Archie, who seemed to be in charge.

"Right," he said when she'd finished. "You've done very well, Miss Anderson. Both Miss Andersons. It's more or less as we'd worked out. There is no time to be lost. The Polaris sub and the anti-mini-sub subs are all in place. We must cut along to Auchmithie."

"There is just one thing," said Sel.

"Yes?" said Archie.

"Wasn't it rather odd they should choose Auchmithie?"

"Odd?" said Archie. "How do you mean?"

"She means odd because we knew Auchmithie as well," said Kate.

"Well, a coincidence perhaps," said Archie, "but not odd at all. Auchmithie happens to be the nearest point to all the rigs they planned to mine."

Two hours later Kate, Sel and Monty were hurrying after Captain Archie along the quay at Auchmithie. It was still only nine o'clock in the morning, and a fresh, clear September day: 14 September. A large naval launch was rocking in the harbour. About half the people in Auchmithie seemed to be out on the quay too.

"Look, Kate," said Sel. "There's Jamie MacFin."

"So it is," said Kate. "Hang on, Monty."

Together they ran over to the little crowd.

"You see, Jamie," said Sel. "I said we'd come back."

"Aye, so you did, Kate – or is it Sel? At least they took some notice of yous two. I went to the police after all when you'd gone and was told to mind me heed."

"Why don't you come with us?" said Kate, adding, "I'm Kate."

Jamie looked excited and embarrassed. "Och, no," he said. "Weel – perhaps if – do you think yon admiral would mind?"

Kate ran after Captain Archie and in a moment was waving at Sel and Jamie to join her. A little later all three were standing on the bridge of the launch with Monty as it sped towards the wrecked tanker.

They stopped a hundred yards from it and at once a message boomed out from the loudspeaker. It was in Chinese.

Nothing stirred on the tanker. A second message had begun when suddenly a little figure appeared on the deck.

"I bet that's the guard," said Kate.

Once more a message in Chinese boomed out over the water, then the launch swung round and raced back towards Auchmithie.

"We've given them a quarter of an hour to surrender," said Captain Archie, leaving his controls for a moment. "A quarter of an hour and then we sink her."

And exactly a quarter of an hour later, they heard the sound of jet engines approaching rapidly from the north. The low-flying bombers came in over the sea, circled once, then roared in across the bay. As they passed over the tanker, a succession of bombs fell into the sea in front of it, exploding in great fountains of water.

At first nothing seemed to have happened. Then they saw that the wrecked tanker was shifting and heaving. Very slowly, it was moving further away, and as it moved, the end nearest the shore rose gradually into the air. Higher and higher it rose and then all at once, with gurgling and bursting sounds that they could hear from the launch, Kate and Sel and Jamie and Monty saw it vanish beneath the waves.

They learned afterwards that all six terrorist min-subs had tried to escape and had been captured. The navy had used the new mini-sub stun torpedoes and automatic deep-sea foiling nets.

That was all later. Now, young Captain Archie said to Monty, "I believe it's Lydd Airport in Kent you guys want, isn't it, Goody?"

"Yes," said Monty.

•

"And are you really still not cross with us?" said Kate.

She was sitting on her father's knee. They had spent all afternoon describing what had happened. Sylvia Anderson moved Sel gently off her knee and went over to the stove.

"No," she said. "We were very worried, and then cross, but it's so wonderful to have you all back,

117

nothing matters at all. Not even your very odd new hairstyles."

"We had to disguise ourselves," said Sel.

"Or we'd have been caught and sent home," said Kate.

"I know," said their mother. "But they're still odd. More tea, Monty?"

"A *soupçon*," said Monty.

"One thing I don't understand," said Kate, "is why you left that note at Le Bijou, Monty. 'Thomé's tomb. Try the rose.' "

"Oh, it was a note to remind me," said Monty. "I was looking for a title for my film. I thought I might call *my* terrorist gang 'The Companions of the Rose'."

"Or 'Companions of the Nose'," said Sel, giggling.

"Yes. Why not, Monty?" said Kate. "Sounds good. 'Companions of the Nose'."

"Perhaps, darling," said Monty, looking rather puzzled.

"What I'd like to know," said Sel, "is this. You know that letter they made you write when you were captured. Well, did you *mean* it to read HELP?"

"Yes, I did," said Monty. "I thought 'Serena' might alert you. Very feeble."

"Sel spotted it," said Kate generously.

"But it was Kate who worked out it *had* to be a person in the golf-bag," said Sel.

"You have both been extremely clever girls,"

said Monty. "And extremely clever girls should go to extremely good schools. I have decided to pay for you both to go to the best girls' school in England – St Laura's in Norfolk."

There was a short, embarrassed silence. The Anderson family all looked at each other. At last Sel said, "A *boarding* school?"

"*Girls*?" said Kate. "No boys?"

"A splendid girls' boarding school and the best in England," said Monty. "Run by my sister, Amelia."

There was another silence. Then David Anderson said, "It's very good of you, Monty, but Sylvia and I had always intended the twins to go to the school at Tenterden. At the same time, I don't want to stand in their way. It's their decision. What do you think, girls?"

"But, David," said Sylvia Anderson, "isn't that the school that's had that murder recently? It was on the telly the other night. They don't know who did it."

"A murder?" cried Monty. "A murder at Amelia's school?"

The twins looked at each other. "A murder?" said Kate. "That rather changes things."

"Yes," said Sel. "Perhaps we should give it a try."

"For a term," said Kate. "We can always leave if we don't like it."

"Yes," said Sel. "I told Kate we needed a body. Murder is really proper. Kidnapping is all very well, and dope and so on, but solving a murder would be much more interesting."

"Yes," said Kate, "much, *much* more interesting."

Sharon Creech
Walk Two Moons

*Just over a year ago, my father plucked me up like a weed
and took me and all our belongings (no, that is not true – he
did not bring the chestnut tree or the willow or the maple or
the hayloft or the swimming hole or any of those things which
belong to me) and we drove three hundred miles straight
north and stopped in front of a house in Euclid, Ohio.*

There, Salamanca Hiddle begins to unravel the mystery that
surrounds her world – a world from which her mother has
suddenly, and without warning, disappeared.

'A powerful, emotional narrative which keeps the reader
guessing right up to the end.'
Smarties Prize judges

'A really satisfying book – funny, poignant, cunning in the
unravelling of its mysteries.'
Observer

Winner of the Newbery Medal
Winner of Children's Book of the Year (Longer Novels)
Shortlisted for the Smarties Book Prize